THE PEACH PIT

PICK UP MORE PEACH ADVENTURES!

Book 1:
When Life Gives You Lemons,
Make Peach Pie

SERVING UP SOON!
Book 3:
Frozen Peaches

THE PEACH PIT

ERIN SODERBERG DOWNING

PIXEL+INK

PIXEL▪▪INK

Printed and bound in February 2022 at Maple Press, York, PA, USA.

Book design and interior illustrations by Michelle Cunningham
Freddy's artwork by Henry Downing

www.pixelandinkbooks.com

First Edition
Library of Congress Cataloging-in-Publication Data

Names: Downing, Erin Soderberg, author.
Title: The Peach Pit / Erin Soderberg Downing.
Description: New York : Pixel+Ink, 2022. | Series: The great peach
experiment ; 2 | Audience: Ages 8-12. | Audience: Grades 4-6. |
Summary: Mayhem ensues when the Peaches are gifted a historic
mansion on the condition that they turn it into a bed-and-breakfast.
Identifiers: LCCN 2021047836 | ISBN 9781645950363 (hardcover) |
ISBN 9781645951018 (ebook)
Subjects: CYAC: Bed and breakfast accommodations—Fiction. |
Dwellings—Remodeling—Fiction. | Family life—Fiction. |
Humorous stories.
Classification: LCC PZ7.1.D6884 Pe 2022 | DDC [Fic]—dc23
LC record available at https://lccn.loc.gov/2021047836
Hardcover ISBN 978-1-64595-036-3
eBook ISBN 978-1-64595-101-8

1 3 5 7 9 10 8 6 4 2

*For all the wonderful teachers
who have welcomed the Peach Pie Truck
into their classrooms. Thank you.*

1

THE CREEPY MANSION

Herb Peach was pretty sure his Great Aunt Lucinda's house was haunted. There was just *something* about the massive red brick mansion that gave him the willies. The Peach family visited their great aunt often, and she herself was always cheerful, friendly, and welcoming. The house? It was not.

Maybe it was the way the hall chandelier cast shadows that looked a lot like screaming little faces. Or how the creaky old stairs and radiators groaned and moaned, even when no one was nearby. Then there were the dusty old portraits hanging on the living room wall, with their painted eyes that seemed to watch Herb whenever he rushed past. He also found it strange that the house always smelled like split pea soup and crackers, even though Great Aunt Lucinda didn't even *like* soup.

Whatever the reason, eight-year-old Herb always felt a little skittish inside his great aunt's big, cold house. He looked forward to the moment their dad would say it was time for his family to pile into the car to head back across town to their own small, comfy house. It was always a relief to get home.

This was unfortunate, since it sounded like his family might be *moving in* to the creaky old mansion.

"Welcome, *welcome!*" Aunt Lucinda flung open the brick mansion's enormous front door. She stepped out onto the front stoop and pulled Herb into a hug, squeezing him so tight that he squeaked a little bit. "I've missed you so much, Herbie muffin!"

"*Mfff mu,* too," Herb said, wriggling out of his great aunt's arms.

Next, Aunt Lucinda turned and kissed Herb's big sister, Lucy, once on each side of her face. "Kisses, kisses, like they do in France, *ma chérie!*" she announced. After offering her great aunt a huge smile and hug in return, twelve-year-old Lucy set to work trying to wipe the bright red lipstick prints off each of her cheeks.

"And look at you," Aunt Lucinda gasped, stepping across the large, covered stone patio. She grabbed ten-year-old Freddy's shoulders before pulling him in for a hug that looked slightly less squeezy than the one Herb had gotten. "You've grown so much over the summer!"

"You should see my toenails," Freddy murmured into Aunt Lucinda's shoulder, his voice muffled by the enormous black-and-silver curly wig Aunt Lucinda had perched atop her head. Aunt Lucinda's hair was never the same, Herb had noticed. She had a seemingly endless collection of wigs that she traded out depending on her mood and outfit.

Herb's dad climbed up the steps and joined his three kids on the mansion's front porch, offering his aunt a formal handshake. Even though Dad had known Aunt Lucinda his whole life—she was *his* aunt, after all—Dad always greeted her like she was some distant relative he only saw at weddings and funerals. Great Aunt Lucinda took his hand in hers and, in a friendly voice, said, "Wally, dear. How are you?"

Herb giggled. No one called their dad *Wally* except Great Aunt Lucinda. Most everyone called him Walter, or Professor Peach (since he was a geology professor at the university in their hometown of Duluth, Minnesota). Herb and his two older siblings just called him *Dad*.

Dad held out a golden-brown peach pie and said, "It's good to see you. We brought a pie." He held it aloft and Herb took a quick step back. Even *looking* at pie still made him feel a little bit queasy. After spending part of the summer traveling around the country with his family, selling pie out of an old, beaten-down food truck,

Herb was pied-out. He never wanted to eat pie again in his entire life.

"Oh, you shouldn't have," Aunt Lucinda said. But even as she said it, Herb watched her tear off a small piece of the pie's crust and pop it in her mouth. She winked at Herb. Before their big summer road trip, the Peaches had visited Great Aunt Lucinda fairly regularly—once a week, usually—and always brought her some sort of little hostess gift. A book, a fake plant, or comfortable socks with funny sayings on them. In exchange, Aunt Lucinda cooked the Peach family delicious homemade meals and had endless supplies of chocolate on hand. "Come in, come in," she said, ushering them inside.

Before Herb had even taken off his shoes, there was an explosion of yaps and barks as four small, energetic dogs skidded into the front entryway. Their tiny toe-nails made pat-a-pat-a-pat sounds as the dogs raced across the hardwood floors. They greeted the Peaches with a lot of barking and jumping, and one of the pups even managed to dip his furry snout in the peach pie Aunt Lucinda had carelessly set on a bench just inside the door.

"Dasher! Get away from my snack," Aunt Lucinda scolded, shooing him away. "Donny, Vix, Rudy—behave!"

Herb plopped down onto the floor and let the dogs

run all over him. He hadn't seen Aunt Lucinda's pups in nearly two months, not since before his family had left for their monthlong great food truck adventure. When they'd finally gotten back to Minnesota at the end of July, Aunt Lucinda was away and the pups were at "camp," which is what their great aunt called the kennel. But now that summer was almost over, everyone was back home in Duluth, and Herb had a lot of missed cuddling and playtime to make up for.

Truth be told, Aunt Lucinda and her dogs were the only things that kept Herb coming back to this big, scary mansion. Aunt Lucinda had always felt more like a grandma to him than a great aunt. Herb's actual grandparents had all passed away long ago, and after their mom died of cancer two years earlier, Dad's Aunt Lucinda had become an even more important part of the Peaches' lives. She was the only other family they really had. And the pups were an added bonus.

Herb squirmed around on the wooden floor, trying to give equal belly rubs and ear scratches to everyone. The four little pups *loved* Herb, and Herb had lots of love to give back. The pups climbed over one another, eagerly sniffing Herb's face, nibbling and tugging at his shirt, and poking their noses into his pockets. Aunt Lucinda's pack of pups was very naughty, but also very sweet.

By the time he had finished giving each of the dogs a proper greeting, Herb noticed that the rest of his family had made their way into Aunt Lucinda's enormous living room. Herb scooped Dasher up into his arms and followed his family. The other three dogs chased after him, leaping onto the sofas and chairs to greet the rest of the family.

Freddy had flopped onto a couch, Lucy was browsing the built-in bookshelves on the far end of the living room, and Aunt Lucinda sat in her recliner next to the unlit fireplace. Dad was perched awkwardly on the front edge of Herb's favorite big, squishy armchair. Herb squeezed in behind Dad, trying to hide from all the paintings that always seemed to be keeping watch over his every move.

"So . . ." Dad said, at the exact same time Aunt Lucinda said, "Well . . ."

Aunt Lucinda chuckled and went on. "I'm guessing you have some questions about my letter."

Dad nodded. When the Peaches had returned from their summer road trip in the Peach Pie Truck, they had found a letter from Great Aunt Lucinda waiting for them in the mailbox of their tiny house across town. It was filled with a bunch of surprises.

The past *summer* had been filled with surprises.

First, the Peach kids had learned that one of their mom's inventions had sold, two whole years after she died—which turned the Peach family into overnight millionaires. Dad had donated most of the money to charity, and saved most of the rest for his kids' college, but he'd also set aside a small sliver of Mom's windfall to spend on "fun stuff." Then, Dad had surprised the kids with the news that he'd bought a used food truck— this, he told them, was what he meant by "fun stuff."

But the biggest shock of all had come when they'd found out Dad was taking a whole month off from work, in order to travel around the Midwest, selling pies as a family. Aunt Lucinda's surprising note had capped off a summer that was full of twists and turns.

Great Aunt Lucinda had been visiting her daughter in Europe when Herb and his family had returned home, so the Peaches had all been waiting impatiently—for nearly all of August—to find out what her unusual letter meant. "Like I said in my letter, I've decided to move into an apartment at the Birch Pond retirement community, and I'm giving you my house," Aunt Lucinda said bluntly. This is what Lucy had *told* Herb the letter said. He'd even read it with his own eyes, but he had a hard time believing it could be true. Who just *gave* someone a *house*?

"Why?" Lucy asked, spinning away from the bookshelves. "You love this house."

"I love this house, yes, but it's a pit," Aunt Lucinda said, gesturing to a patch of peeling wallpaper and the light switch that everyone in the family knew didn't work. "It's too much for me to keep up. And frankly, I'm lonely. All I've got is these dogs to keep me company day in and day out, and I'm just not putting the place to good use."

"So, what are you saying? You want us to . . . put the place to good use?" Dad asked. "What does that mean, exactly?"

"Move in. Make it great again and bring the place back to life—" Before Aunt Lucinda could finish what she was saying, a loud clank sounded somewhere upstairs. Then something clunked and vibrated inside the walls. The dogs all started barking at once, and Herb squeezed in closer to his dad.

"That's just the ghost upstairs," Aunt Lucinda explained with a casual laugh. "One of many, as you know. You'll get used to all the racket they make."

Herb gulped. Aunt Lucinda had joked about her house ghosts before, but Herb had never really paid much attention. After all, he'd never had to *sleep* in the mansion alongside all those funny noises. But now it was sounding like . . . that might be changing?

He looked around the room, taking it all in with fresh eyes. The creepy shadows on the walls, eyes staring out from the artwork, the spooky noises, secret passageways, and dark corners. *Home sweet home.*

2

· · · · · · · · · · · · · · · · · ·

HANDING OVER THE KEYS

Lucy Peach didn't know what to say. Who just *gave* someone a house? Aunt Lucinda, that's who. One of the things Lucy had always loved most about her great aunt was that she didn't seem to do things the way most people did. She was eccentric, and this surprise news about *giving* the Peaches her mansion proved it. Lucy also loved that she and her great aunt shared a name: Lucinda. It was majestic and having the same name made Lucy feel like they were connected somehow. Lucy liked thinking that someday she might grow up to be a lot like Great Aunt Lucinda.

"What do you mean, you want us to make your house great again?" Lucy asked, hustling across the enormous living room. Her little brother Herb had always been creeped out by Aunt Lucinda's mansion, and she could tell that the crack about ghosts hadn't helped *at all*. Lucy plucked one of the dogs off the floor and plopped it into the chair beside Herb and Dad. The pup licked and sniffed Herb's face, which Lucy hoped would distract her brother from the alarming sounds in the walls.

Aunt Lucinda chuckled. "This place has turned into an utter *pit*," she said. "Wobbly banisters, broken door handles, too many rooms that no one's used for years. There could be a whole family of mice living in the fourth-floor bedrooms for all I know." Lucy noticed her brother Freddy cringe when she said this. Freddy wasn't scared of much, but he *hated* mice. Aunt Lucinda sighed. "I never even get up to the third or fourth floor anymore. What I'd like you to do is move in, give this place some love, and fill it with family and life again."

"But," Lucy's dad said, "we *have* a house."

"True," Aunt Lucinda agreed. "But your house is small for three growing kids. And let's face it, this one is better."

No one could argue with that. Even though the Peaches' house was cozy and comfortable enough, it *was* small. But more importantly, Lucy and her siblings had all agreed that it never felt quite *right* after their mom died. Sure, there were good memories of happy times in their little house, but for the past few years, it had also felt like something was missing. Maybe moving into Aunt Lucinda's mansion would be the perfect next step for the Peaches, who'd been desperately trying to make a fresh start as a new kind of family.

A family without Mom, but a *family* nonetheless. The summer working together as a family in the Peach Pie Truck had been challenging and frustrating, but it had also been fun. Even more importantly, it had proven that the Peaches were capable of rebuilding after everything fell apart.

"Do you expect me to buy this place from you?" Dad asked. Lucy's head swiveled from him to their great aunt. "Because we don't have much left." Lucy knew her dad had donated most of the money their mom had earned from the sale of her solar cling invention. He'd also socked away some in college savings accounts for Lucy and her brothers. Dad had recently shifted his schedule so he could work fewer hours, and she knew (thanks to Freddy eavesdropping when he shouldn't have been) that Dad had taken a bit of a pay cut. So even though they'd been millionaires for a minute, money was once again tight. "There's a little bit left over from the sale of the Peach Pie Truck, but—"

Great Aunt Lucinda cut him off. "It's a gift. With conditions."

"What about . . . *David*?" Dad asked, scratching the tufty hair on the top of his head. Unlike the three Peach kids, who all had thick dark hair like their mom's, Dad had wispy, pale hair that had been getting thinner with each passing year. "Won't he want the house?"

"Who's David?" Freddy asked. While the others talked, Freddy had been carefully using a felt-tip pen to turn the scab on his shin into a piece of art. The scab now blended in as one of many planets in a solar system that Freddy had drawn on his entire lower leg.

Lucy rolled her eyes and plunked down on the sofa next to her brother. "David *Peach*," she blurted out. "Dad's cousin? Aunt Lucinda's *son*?"

"Oh," Freddy said with a shrug. "That guy."

"*That guy*," Aunt Lucinda said, smirking, "lives in California and has no interest in moving back to Duluth. And Renee—my daughter; I think you kids met her once?—she's got her life in Europe. If I were to give either of them the house, they'd just turn around and sell it. In fact, David's trying to bully me into thinking that would be the sensible thing to do. But sensible *schmensible*. Who's got time for that?"

Dad frowned. "Sensible generally makes a lot of sense."

"Eh," Aunt Lucinda waved a hand in the air. Then

she snapped her fingers and said, "Fred, hon, can you grab a fork from the kitchen and hand over that pie you brought for me? I'm just gonna eat it straight out of the pan. A plate would be *sensible*, but it wouldn't taste half as good as just diving right in. I *am* the one who created this peach pie recipe to begin with, so I get to decide for myself how I want to eat it."

Lucy giggled. Her dad, meanwhile, looked uncomfortable with this plan of attack.

As soon as she had her pie on her lap and fork in hand, Aunt Lucinda said, "So here's the deal." They all waited while she scooped a bite of pie right out of the very middle of the pan. She chewed, then went on. "I've got a few conditions that come along with giving you the house."

"That makes sense," Dad said.

"Shush, now," Aunt Lucinda scolded. "I heard all about what the four of you did with that old food truck this summer. Now I want you to take my old house and make it shine, just the way you did with the Peach Pie Truck. This place has decades of family history, and I'm not ready to see it go. And besides, I think you four will have some fun with it."

"There's probably not a lot we can do," Freddy said suddenly. "Isn't your house on the National Register of

Historic Places?" Though ten-year-old Freddy always claimed to be the not-so-smart Peach, he had a whole lot of facts and information stuffed into his body. But how on earth did he know *that*, Lucy wondered?

"That it is," Aunt Lucinda said. "My house was even featured in a book about Midwest mansions back in the eighties."

"What does *National Register* mean?" Herb asked.

"It basically means my house has to be preserved in a special way, because it's considered a historic treasure," Lucinda said. "It hasn't been changed much since it was first built over a century ago. Now, no one is allowed to tear important stuff down or change the look of it much. But what you *can* do is polish it up and share it with others." She took another bite of pie, closed her eyes, and said quietly, "Do you remember how much Madeline loved this house?"

Lucy nodded. Before she died, and even when she'd been really sick, her mom had *loved* visiting Aunt Lucinda and her mansion. She was always ooh-ing and ahh-ing over the little artistic details that were carved into the woodwork, and she loved playing hide-and-seek with Lucy in the hidden staircases. She and Great Aunt Lucinda had been partners for a confusing card game called Bridge that they played with some other ladies a few times each month, and Mom liked coming over to practice her fix-it skills when stuff broke or fell apart in the mansion. But Mom had especially loved reading in the window seat on the first-floor stair landing.

"Walter," Great Aunt Lucinda said, snapping Lucy out of her memories, "think of all the times your wife talked about what a lovely bed-and-breakfast this home would make. Which is why I've decided that's what I want you to do. I want the four of you to live here and turn it into a B and B. The time has come to share this wonderful house with others."

Dad shook his head. "I don't understand," he said. "I don't know the first thing about bed-and-breakfasts."

All Lucy knew was that they were a little like a hotel, except smaller, and they had free breakfast in the morning.

"You didn't know squat about pie," Aunt Lucinda pointed out. "Or food trucks, either. But you made that work. You're four smart cookies, so I trust you can figure this out, too. It's gonna be good for you. A way to build a new home for your new family, together."

Freddy had bounced out of the sofa and was now pacing back and forth in front of it. "Okay, lemme get this straight," he said. "You want us to move in here, fix things up, and start renting out rooms to turn this creepy old mansion into a bed-and-breakfast?"

"Exactly." Aunt Lucinda took another bite of pie,

then gently set the pan down on the ground. The dogs swarmed, gobbling up what was left before licking the pan clean.

"Phase Two of the Great Peach Experiment!" Freddy whooped. "This is *perfect*. And I can finally have my very own room—no more sharing with Herb."

Herb clearly hadn't thought of this yet. Now, Lucy's littlest brother looked torn between the horror of moving into the spooky old mansion they had previously only *visited* and the freedom of having a bedroom all to himself. Lucy already knew exactly which room in Aunt Lucinda's house she'd want to move into. There was a small bedroom on the fourth floor with a whole wall of bookshelves and a giant closet with a little sitting nook in the middle of one wall. The closet would be perfect for a reading fort, and she could display all her books on the shelves for easy browsing.

"I'm going to lay it all out there," Great Aunt Lucinda blurted. "This big house isn't cheap to heat through the winter, and the property taxes cost enough to knock a person on their butt. I'll help out by covering those expenses for a few months, but at that point you'll need to sell your current house to cover the costs. No way you can hold onto both."

Lucy swallowed a lump that had formed in her throat. *Get rid of their house?*

"If we're going to be living here, I'd need to rent out our other house to students or something," Dad said quietly. "I don't want the pipes to freeze, and it seems wasteful to have that place sit empty."

"Whatever you decide," Great Aunt Lucinda said quietly. "If it doesn't work out, it doesn't work out, and you go back to the way things were."

While the kids chewed on the plan, Lucy noticed Dad had gone a bit pale. He was now muttering to himself and looked a little panicked. Clearly, Aunt Lucinda had also noticed. "Wally, I wouldn't have considered this as an option if I didn't think you were up to it. And frankly, this house has been as much a part of your life as anyone else's."

Aunt Lucinda stood up, looking very regal as she addressed the three Peach kids. "Did you kids know that your dad used to spend a lot of summers here in Duluth with my family? I know he's told you about some of the trips we used to take. But after our travels, we'd all settle in back here and he and my kids—your dad's cousins—would play together around the house and explore the neighborhood the rest of the summer. Your father and his dad moved around a lot for your grandpop's job in the army, but this house was always kind of his home base."

Dad smiled. "Those were happy summers. I do love this house."

Lucy loved seeing her dad smile. He'd been sad so much of the past few years, ever since Mom died, and it still felt new and unusual to see him happy again. During their summer in the Peach Pie Truck, Dad had told his kids stories about some of his summer adventures with Aunt Lucinda and Uncle Martin, after his own mom passed away when he was about Lucy's age. But Lucy hadn't realized Duluth had been a kind of home for him as a kid. Dad's childhood hadn't been easy, and it sounded like this house had been the one thing that hadn't changed from year to year. Lucy could see how that would be a welcome thing to look forward to every summer.

"So," Aunt Lucinda said in a tone that meant business, "you have until Thanksgiving to figure out how to make it work, and then I need to make some big decisions. David's been talking to an eager buyer who says he'll give us until December first to figure out if we're interested in selling. I'll move all my personal effects out of here this week, and you all can move in and get started planning. Lucy already told me you still have a little of that pot of fun money left over from Madeline's solar cling invention after selling the Peach Pie Truck, so I figured you could use some of that to hire people to fix some things up. Your wife would have definitely loved to see you spend some of her money on a project like this."

"Mom would totally approve of this plan," Lucy agreed. "She always wanted to open a B and B, and this house was one of her favorite places on earth."

Aunt Lucinda winked at her. "David is coming to Duluth for a visit over Thanksgiving. The two of us will plan to stay at your B and B to see how things have come along. I'll keep away until then, so I can be *wowed* by the big reveal." She plopped a giant, old-fashioned key to the mansion into Lucy's lap. It was cold and curved and golden, and Lucy wanted nothing more than to keep it forever. The key made her feel more hopeful than she had in a very long time.

"What if we can't get it figured out by then?" Dad asked. "That's not a lot of time to turn an old house into a B and B. We need to pack, and move, and I've got work to consider . . ."

Lucy agreed. It *wasn't* a lot of time. But they'd turned the Peach Pie Truck into a success—sort of. Maybe this wasn't so crazy? How amazing would it be if they *could* make Aunt Lucinda's plan work? The key to a dream home, a place to start building their new life together as a family, had literally just been dropped in their laps.

Aunt Lucinda shrugged. "If the bed-and-breakfast is good to go by Thanksgiving, I'll transfer the title of the house to you for good. If it's *not* working out, I'll need to sell this place—and all the memories wrapped up inside—to a stranger. But I have faith in you, Peaches. Don't let me down."

Dear Aunt Lucinda,

   If we're going to be running a Bed & Breakfast out of the Peach Pit (sorry, that's what Freddy's been calling the mansion ever since he heard you describe it as a pit), hopefully all our pie-baking skills from this summer will come in handy again! Can we serve pie to the guests for breakfast?

Much love,
Lucy

PS: Here's your recipe back—I made a few adjustments.

Lucinda's Famous Peach Pie Recipe

Ingredients:

- 4–5 cups peeled and sliced peaches (5–8 peaches, depending on how big they are)
    * frozen works just fine, if you thaw them and drain the liquid after
- 1/2 C sugar (more or less to your taste)
- 1/4 C brown sugar
- 3–4 tablespoons cornstarch or flour (to thicken)
- 2 teaspoons lemon or key lime juice (orange juice could work in a pinch—just need the acid!)
- 2–3 T melted butter
- 1/2 t cinnamon
- 1/4–1/2 t nutmeg
- A healthy dash of cardamom & salt

1. Mix up sugar and fruit, then let that mix sit while you get your crusts ready*
    * Crust recipe on reverse. Roll out half your crust dough to cover the bottom of your pie pan, and use whatever you like for the top: lattice top, crumb topping, double crust

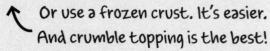 Or use a frozen crust. It's easier. And crumble topping is the best!

2. Preheat oven to 375–400° F (temp depends on your oven—mine's finnicky). While it warms up, mix the fruit/sugar combo with the cornstarch and juice, then add the remaining ingredients.

3. Pour everything into your crust and figure out your choice of topping. Wrap the pie edges loosely with strips of foil so your crust doesn't burn. Bake about 40 minutes; peel off the foil. Bake until it's bubbly and the crust is nice and brown, maybe 10–20 minutes longer.

4. Cool, then top with plenty of ice cream.

LUCY'S CRUMB TOPPING RECIPE

- 1/3 C sugar
- 1/3 C brown sugar
- 3/4 C flour
- 1/2–2/3 C cold butter cut into chunks
- Dash of cinnamon or pumpkin pie spice
- Optional: Some oats, to make it healthier (?)

1. Mix all these ingredients together on the pulse setting of a food processor, or cut it all together by hand with two knives or a pastry chopper.

3

PLAN, PREP, PACK & PIZZA

Freddy was what other kids at camp called a "master builder." For the third year in a row, he was taking part in a weeklong Cardboard Camp that took over one of Duluth's sprawling parks during the last days of summer break. All day long, for five days, nearly a hundred kids designed and built an enormous castle made out of wood (the frame) and cardboard (the walls), constructed weapons and armor from cardboard and paper-mache, and worked in teams to plot missions and battles and form alliances (alliances that oftentimes carried on into the school year).

"Hand me that skinny piece," Freddy called out to his friend Ethan, who was assisting Freddy with the castle build. Freddy was standing a good twelve feet off the ground, on wooden and metal scaffolding that was in the process of being converted into a cardboard-covered fortress. Ethan tossed the requested strip of cardboard up to Freddy, who nailed it in place. Meanwhile, Henry, the boys' other friend, came racing toward them with a bucket of paint and a brush swinging at his side. They'd use the paint to mark this part of the castle with their group's logo, in order to lay claim to the newest corner of the fortress.

Freddy loved Cardboard Camp, and was relieved that his family's trip in the Peach Pie Truck hadn't interfered with his favorite week of summer break. He loved helping to plan and design and build a new cardboard fortress each year. Even when his two best friends and the rest of their camp group set off on adventures to search for counselors' hidden relics in the woods on the outskirts of the park during the day, Freddy stuck close to the castle and kept building. The castle at Cardboard Camp was one of the places he felt most alive.

Ten-year-old Freddy had always loved building and inventing and creating stuff, and he could hardly believe his luck a few days earlier, when Great Aunt Lucinda had told his family she was giving them a real, actual, genuine *mansion* and letting them fix it up. This project would be like Cardboard Camp times a million. Turning Great Aunt Lucinda's so-called Peach Pit into a castle fit for guests was Freddy's dream come true.

The past week had been a whirlwind. Fifth grade

would be starting up in just a few days, and Freddy couldn't think of a better way to spend his final hours of freedom. All day long, he got to be outside at Cardboard Camp with his best friends, and afterward he worked on packing up his half of a bedroom and the giant mess of art supplies he'd picked up from all around the house. School (which was *not* Freddy's favorite) started Monday, and the Peaches had a *lot* to do to get themselves moved and settled into their new space before then.

"Check this out!" Henry whooped as he charged up the wooden stairs of the castle. "I got us paint *and* I found the silver egg!" He held a giant, tinfoil-wrapped blob over his head and grinned. "Isn't it beautiful?"

"We can trade that in for six extra boxes," Freddy cheered. All week, groups of campers hunted for hidden treasures ("relics") that counselors had tucked into various corners of the sprawling park. When found, the treasures could be traded for raw materials kids could use to build weapons and add extra rooms to the castle. "I still need to build a latrine for our wing of the castle!"

"We don't need a toilet," Ethan pointed out. "Who wants to 'go' in a cardboard pee pot?"

"A toilet is the heart of a home," Freddy explained. "It's the one spot in a castle that everyone has in common."

"Besides, what kind of castle *doesn't* have a bath-room?" Henry argued. "I'm with Freddy on this one."

"But I really need to buy supplies to make full-body armor," Ethan argued. "The bubble troll is supposed to make a guest appearance during the final battle tomor-row, and I need to be ready to fight him off."

The boys bickered and chatted about their battle plan and what they most wanted to buy with their sil-ver egg, while making their way toward the central battlefield for afternoon farewell. Camp was over for the day, and it was time for Freddy to head home and finish packing.

As soon as he'd collected his stuff and said good-bye to his friends and campmates, Freddy biked a couple miles over and three long blocks uphill to get home. On the way, he thought about how weird it would be that *next* summer he'd be biking the other direction and *down* the hill to get to his new house. That was assum-ing, of course, that his family could make Aunt Lucinda's B&B plan work, which Freddy was sure was possible.

How hard could it be to fix up their great aunt's dusty old house and turn it into a welcome space for guests? It couldn't be any more challenging than run-ning a food truck. During this past summer, the Peaches had become *experts* at building new businesses and after slinging pie all summer, this next Great Peach Experiment should be easy-peasy.

As soon as he got home, however, Freddy remembered what it was like to work with his family. His dad, specifically. At that moment, Freddy's actual, verified genius-of-a-dad was squatting inside a giant moving container in the driveway. The massive crate, which had been parked outside for nearly three days now, was completely empty save one lone box in the far back corner. As a scientist, Dad was big on planning—he embarked on almost every project using the scientific method:

1. Ask a question
2. Do background research
3. Construct a hypothesis
4. Test with an experiment
5. Is the procedure working? If no, repeat steps 1–4. If yes, carry on.
6. Analyze data and draw conclusions
7. Do the results align with the hypothesis?
8. Analyze and communicate results

Unfortunately, Dad was trying to use the scientific method to figure out the best way to pack up their house for the big move. This meant he'd been doing endless testing and measuring to try to come up with the most efficient way to fit everything into the moving container. Most of the family's boxes were packed and ready to go, and they'd decided which pieces of furniture and larger items (the stuff that didn't fit in boxes) they wanted to take along. But nothing had actually made it *from* the house *to* the moving container, because Dad couldn't just load and go without making a big, fat deal out of the whole process.

And they weren't even taking everything! Dad had decided it made the most sense to rent their house to some graduate students he knew from work until they found out if they would get to keep Aunt Lucinda's mansion forever. Dad had rented it to the students partially furnished (since Great Aunt Lucinda's mansion already *had* furniture), so there wasn't even a whole lot of stuff to load. Much as Freddy didn't like the idea of some smelly twenty-year-old sleeping in his bunk bed, he also didn't like the idea of their house being left empty. He had read a story about a house in Alaska or Canada or Maine that had been left empty one winter, and all the water pipes froze, burst, and turned the house into a sort of ice castle. As cool as it would be to spend the night in an ice castle (like the Ice Hotel made every year in the north of Sweden!), Freddy didn't want that to happen to his house.

As he watched Dad measure and futz inside the crate, Freddy realized it was time for him to step in, or this move was going to take an eternity. "Dad . . ." he said carefully, not wanting to startle the old guy when he was in the middle of a thought. "You know everything we're planning to take will fit in here easily. There's more than enough space in the crate, with room to spare."

"I know that, Freddy," Dad snapped. "But why would you want to waste space and time just tossing stuff into the crate willy-nilly, when we could plan first and do this as efficiently as possible?"

Freddy sighed. Though their dad had begun to learn to relax and go with the flow (more than anyone could ever have imagined possible) during their summer road trip, he still had his quirks and unique ways of doing things. Luckily, during the time they'd all spent together squished into a tiny food truck and two tents all summer, Freddy had begun to figure out how to manage him. "Weren't you supposed to go to work this afternoon for a meeting with your grad students?"

Walter Peach was a geology professor, but he also ran a lab and helped oversee a bunch of student research at the university where he worked. He'd taken the summer off to travel around with his kids and spend more time doing some fun stuff together back home in Duluth, but now he was starting to ease back into work. He'd explained to Freddy, Lucy, and Herb that their family couldn't afford for him *not* to work at all (and also Dad *loved* work), but after they got back from their summer adventure, he had promised them he would focus on improving his work-home life balance. He was even seeing a therapist to help him work through some emotions and other stuff he hadn't really paid much attention to after their mom died, which Freddy thought was pretty cool. It was a big step for their dad.

Because he liked having Dad around more, Freddy had every intention of making him keep his promise; but right now, it would be best if his dad would focus more on work for a bit and leave the home stuff to his kids. Dad looked up in surprise. "Oh, my meeting! What time is it?"

"Four." Freddy's stomach growled at the reminder that it was also afternoon-snack time.

"Oh dear," Dad said, shaking his head. "I need to hustle."

"While you're gone, Lucy and Herb and I can start loading boxes up. Tomorrow afternoon is move day, right?"

"Tomorrow?" Dad frowned. "I don't think we'll be ready for that."

"School starts Monday," Freddy reminded him. "We need the weekend to unpack and stuff."

"We'll see," Dad said absentmindedly. Then he headed off without another word.

Freddy knew that if he and his siblings put a couple hours of work in to getting their boxes loaded tonight, they'd be plenty ready. Aunt Lucinda was already settled into her new apartment, so her home was pretty much ready for them. Lucy and Herb had spent several hours at the house (their new mansion!) over the past few days, to visit the dogs. The pups were currently living in the Peach Pit with a dog-sitter, waiting for their new family to arrive. "The pups come with the house," Aunt Lucinda had explained when she handed over the keys to their new palace. "I can't have pets at my new apartment, and besides, this pack needs more attention and exercise than I can give 'em."

After inhaling three bowls of cereal, Freddy set out to find his siblings. In their shared bedroom, Herb was carefully loading his various collections into towel-lined boxes (Freddy's little brother had a collection of *pine cones* that he treated with as much love and care as he would a live animal). "Want to take a break to help load up the moving crate?" Freddy asked. "With me and Lucy?"

Herb wasn't excited about the move, so he'd been moving *slooooowly* through his packing (almost as slow as the world's slowest mammal, which Freddy happened to know was the three-toed sloth). But Freddy knew Herb loved being included in his older siblings' plans, so he wasn't surprised when Herb leaped right up with a jolly "Sure!"

Lucy's best friend, Maren, had been over at the house all day helping Lucy pack her stuff, and said she would also be happy to haul some boxes out to the crate. This was good news—Maren was a swimmer, and Freddy had always been jealous of her insane arm and shoulder muscles.

Knowing extra help would make everything easier and more fun, Freddy called both Ethan and Henry, hoping *his* best friends would also be willing to come over and schlep some boxes. They said yes only after Freddy promised his dad would feed them pizza afterward. (He'd figure out how to get Dad on board with this plan later.)

The work was hard and tedious, but the Peach house was small, so it didn't take long to make a big dent in the stack of stuff that was packed up and ready to go. By the time their dad returned home from his meeting, the six kids had loaded all but five of the packed boxes into the moving crate. There were just a few half-full boxes, a couple pieces of furniture, and several clunky wardrobe boxes left to get, and then they'd be done. With the majority of their stuff inside the crate, the moving pod was still half empty. No scientific method would be necessary to get everything to fit.

"W-wow," Dad stuttered, clearly shocked by how much his kids had done while he was gone. The thing Dad *still* hadn't seemed to fully realize, Freddy knew, was that the Peach kids had been running the family pretty much on their own for the past two years. Ever since their mom died and Dad had kind of disappeared into his sadness, the kids had been forced to keep things together. They'd adapted, figured out how to fend for themselves, and had learned the value of a we'll-get-through-this-together attitude. These skills (along with Lucy's excellent organizational ability and annoying oldest-kid bossiness) had gotten them through some very tough years. It was the kids who'd made their summer Peach Pie Truck experiment a success. Over the past summer, Dad had changed a lot—but he still had a lot to learn about what his kids were capable of doing.

Freddy had been a big part of his family's victory

during the summer Great Peach Experiment, and he had every intention of making this next phase of the experiment just as successful. But this time, the stakes had been raised; there was a whole *mansion* on the line. A private bedroom for everyone. Room in the driveway for a basketball hoop (or maybe a pool for Herb?). Plenty of space to spread out and work on art projects. A house that was *begging* for his family's clever brains and Freddy's creative ideas.

There was a whole new kind of *life* waiting for them on the other side of town. A house-sized blank canvas, all prepped and primed to be turned into a masterpiece. While he'd worked on planning and building the castle at Cardboard Camp that week, Freddy had had plenty of time to think about what his family could do with Great Aunt Lucinda's castle. He'd always dreamed of designing and fixing up the perfect treehouse fort—but a whole mansion was even better. Freddy had ideas; *lots* of ideas.

Tomorrow, in their grand new home, he could start putting his grand plan in motion.

But first: "Hey, Dad?" Freddy said, flashing his most charming smile. "Remember earlier today when you said we could order pizza tonight? I'll order, if you pay. Deal?"

From the Sketchbook of Freddy Peach:

WHAT CAN YOU GROW OUT OF A PEACH PIT?

Oops, that's brownie

THE DUMP

Freddy's Dream Treehouse!

Junk

Garbage

Lanmans Epic Washer

$$$

Garbage

Fluffy Seat

Trash

Peach Pit

4

A HIDDEN SURPRISE

For Lucy, a normal last-weekend-of-summer schedule would include a lot of reading, sleeping in, a few outings to the city pool or creek or Park Point to go swimming with friends, and plenty of time spent organizing her school binder and supplies. This summer, however, everything *normal* had gone right out the window and it had been *exhausting*. Which is the reason Lucy's first day of seventh grade was fueled by a whole lot of yawns and a stolen, disgusting cup of Dad's morning coffee.

At lunch on her first day back at East Middle School, Lucy slid into her usual spot at a long table with some of her friends and rested her chin in her hands. She stifled another yawn, then sleepily pulled out her sandwich and chocolate milk. Even though she thought coffee tasted like the bottom of an old shoe, and soda made her burp, she kind of wished she had *something* with caffeine that might help her stay awake.

"You okay?" Maren asked, looking concerned.

"I'm great! Just tired," Lucy explained, yawning through a smile. It felt wonderful to be back at school and back to a normal routine. But the crazy schedule and hard work in the food truck this summer, and lack of sleep and *more* hard work during the move this past weekend had all been totally worth it. She was exhausted from the weekend's move, but beyond happy.

"How's the new house?" Lucy's friend Neva asked from across the table.

"It's completely insane," Lucy said. "Great Aunt Lucinda's mansion is *literally* a national treasure, and for now, at least, it's *our* treasure." Even though the Peaches had only been living in the mansion for three nights, Lucy already felt like a princess living in a fairy tale. She couldn't believe the past four months were part of her actual life. They'd gone from an ordinary, no-frills, brainy family to food truck businesspeople to a family that lives in a *mansion* . . . in a matter of months! "Herb hates me right now, though, because I took the bedroom he wanted."

"Poor Herbie," Maren said. Every single one of Lucy's friends loved Herb. Her little brother was charming and funny and sweet and smart . . . and just young enough that all the seventh graders tended to treat him like a baby, which Herb did *not* appreciate. But he *did* love all the bonus older-sister love and attention, so he usually tolerated it. "Why did you steal the poor little guy's room?"

"It's the room I wanted, too! It's perfect for me, and even better, it's on a separate floor from Freddy's," Lucy said. Before they started unloading any of their boxes, they had all picked rooms so they could unload stuff into the right places and not have to move it again later. There were seven bedrooms in total at the Peach Pit (which was the temporary name Freddy had given their new home). They'd talked about how to split all the rooms up, and Freddy pointed out that if they saved enough rooms to have *three* guest rooms, that would mean as many as six extra people (and maybe a baby or two) could be wandering around their house, waiting to be fed, at any given time. That was all any of them thought they could handle.

And so, the three largest bedrooms, all with attached private bathrooms—two on the second floor and one on the third floor—were being reserved for future B&B guests. Dad got the next pick and chose a medium-sized room with a tiny, private balcony on the third floor. The kids then got to pick their rooms in age order. Lucy explained, "I got first pick, since I'm the oldest. I chose the tiniest bedroom, way up on the fourth floor, with built-in bookshelves and a huge closet that has a little alcove tucked into one wall that I can turn into a reading nook."

Herb had wanted that room, too, so he'd have a place to display all his treasures. But Lucy took it, even after Herb tried to say he'd "dibs'ed it." Freddy took the giant bedroom on the third floor, next to Dad, where he'd have plenty of room to lay out his art installations and creations. Herb got last pick and ended up in the other smallish bedroom on the fourth floor, where he'd share a bathroom with Lucy. He'd been sulking ever since, even though Lucy had pointed out that *any* bedroom would be better than the tiny space he'd shared with Freddy in their old house.

"It's strange living in such a giant house," Lucy said. "If you're in the kitchen or living room and need to ask someone a question, you can't just yell and expect them to hear." She didn't want to sound like she was bragging about living in a mansion, but she knew her friends would want all the details and understood that this whole situation was just as crazy to Lucy as it was to all of them. "But get this: the house has an intercom."

"Nuh-uh," June said, a tiny piece of lettuce falling out of her open mouth.

"Yep," Lucy said. "And there are all these old servant staircases, which shows how long the house has been around. So I can go up or down the big, wide staircase in the middle of the house, or slink down these tiny passageways in between some of the rooms and walls." She laughed. "Freddy thinks the servant stairs are epic, but he refuses to use them, because he said they remind him too much of mouse holes and hideouts. And Herb thinks creepy things are waiting to jump out at him from pretty much everywhere. I'm the only one who ever uses the servant staircases, which is pretty cool. It's like they're my own secret passageway."

"Do you get to live in this house forever?" Neva asked, munching on a carrot stick.

"Maybe?" Lucy said. She explained the deal they'd made with Great Aunt Lucinda—that they had to turn it into a working B&B, or she'd let her son sell the place to the highest bidder and the Peaches would go back to their old life.

"Does your family know *anything* about how to run a bed-and-breakfast?" June laughed. "Or how to fix old houses?"

"No," Lucy sighed. "But we didn't know anything about food trucks, either, and somehow we sort of figured it out? Anyway, we're going to hire a few people who can help with some things—a carpenter and a plumber; and then someone who will be around to check guests in, make breakfast, or give people directions when we're all busy, that sort of thing."

"Like a butler?" Maren said, wide-eyed.

"Not a butler." Lucy laughed. "More like . . . a host. Someone who greets guests, and takes money, and is just kind of . . . *around* to help out. Just so we're not stuck at the Peach Pit *all* the time. I don't really know what this person's job would be; Freddy and Dad have already started doing some research on how these kinds of businesses work, and I guess they have a few things figured out. I just know we all want to help out as much as we can, since we got pretty good at customer service this summer and it seems like it would be kind of fun to run a hotel. You know?"

Lucy and her friends talked about the mansion and their plans for the B&B for a while longer, and then they compared their class schedules, listened to cute stories about Neva's new kitten, Maren's summer swim team crush, and—after some discussion—everyone agreed it was totally awful that June's dads had forced her to practice Spanish on some app for thirty minutes every day, all summer long.

Before Lucy had even finished her sandwich, it was

time for fifth-hour Language Arts, which was Lucy's favorite class of the whole day. After Language Arts, Gym, and World Studies, the day was done.

Now that the family was back from their big summer trip, and they were (partly) moved into their new house, and school had started back up again, Lucy felt like her life was kind of getting back on track. After a few strange and sad (and also sometimes wonderful) years, it felt good to see things heading back toward normal. Their family's *new* normal.

As soon as the final bell rang, Lucy hustled home. The middle school finished an hour before the elementary school, and she cherished the time she was home by herself before her dad got home from work and her brothers both swept in. But when she got to the house that afternoon, her dad's car was there and there were also two giant trucks parked outside in the giant driveway. Dad had set up meetings with a bunch of plumbers and electricians and some carpenters that week so they could start to figure out what kind of work needed to be done and how much it might all cost. The Peaches didn't have a lot of money, but they did have the small pot of cash left over from the sale of the food truck. Lucy didn't know a whole lot about home renovation, but she knew it cost a lot. Dad kept arguing that they could do much of the work themselves to save money, but Lucy wasn't so sure. The mansion was in pretty rough shape, and if they were going to have *strangers* paying money to stay there, it would need a lot of help.

If the house were human, Lucy had decided, they would need to give it one of those serious facelift surgeries, instead of just trying to dress it up with makeup.

Inside the back door, Lucy greeted the dogs and waved to her dad. He was standing in the kitchen looking over some papers alongside a man wearing an Al's Plumbing cap. As she grabbed a snack out of the big walk-in pantry, two women with measuring tapes wandered through the dining room next door. Lucy could hear someone (or something) banging around somewhere above her on the second floor. There was a clank and a clatter from above, then someone cursed loud enough that she could hear it echo through the floor.

The dogs raced around from group to group, and up and down the main staircase from the first to the second floor, adding to the chaos. The pack was usually kept contained in one of the small front rooms of the mansion—the "piano" room—during the day to keep them out of trouble, but whoever got home first let them out to potty and roam free. Usually that was Lucy or Herb's job (even if Freddy beat his siblings home, he'd forget to let the dogs out). But today, Dad had released the beasts and they were absolutely zoomy.

As Lucy went to close the pantry closet, the doorknob popped off in her hand and clunked onto the floor. Cringing, she quietly set the fallen knob on a counter inside the pantry and left the door yawning open. The next few months were obviously going to be a little nutso.

Lucy raced upstairs to her new bedroom with the dogs close on her heels. Today, she finally had time to clean and set up her special closet space. Even with a room of her own, Lucy sometimes needed a place she could go and truly hide out from the world. She had plans to turn the giant closet into a cushioned reading nook where she could get lost inside the worlds of her books. She'd need a space where she could find some peace and quiet during the noisy construction work she knew was in their future!

She had spent much of the weekend working on her room—carefully deep-cleaning everything, since no one had really used either of the bedrooms on the fourth floor in years—and got her bed put together and bookshelves organized. She had been saving the closet nook for last, since it was the project she was most excited about. There were a couple boxes and an old rug rolled up inside the closet, so she dragged all those things out and surveyed the special space. The light in the closet didn't work, so she turned on her phone's flashlight to illuminate things. That's when she noticed a small door, way up high in the ceiling. The door was accessible from the nook Lucy had been so excited about, which was more like a ledge that had been built into one wall of the closet.

Curious, Lucy climbed up onto the ledge and pushed up on the door in the ceiling with both hands. At first it wouldn't budge. But when she stood up, stooped slightly in the cramped space, and pushed her shoulder against the little door, it creaked open. Finally, with a pop, it released and fell off to the side inside the open area overhead. Lucy stood up all the way and pressed onto her tiptoes to peek inside the hidden space above her bedroom. Her eyes went wide.

Through the little door was an attic. But not just *any* attic. This attic was *huge*, the size of the entire fourth story of the house, probably, and the beamed ceilings were surprisingly high. Dusty sunlight slivered in from filthy windows on each end of the room, making it easy for Lucy to get a good look around.

There were boxes upon boxes, piles and bins of what looked like Christmas decorations, some old toys and games, a few pieces of raggedy furniture, and a whole lot more. Lucy closed her eyes and said a silent thank-you to the universe. Because she suddenly had more than a reading nook in her closet; she had a whole attic to explore and make her own. Lucy was beginning to think Great Aunt Lucinda's mansion might turn out to be even better than she ever could have imagined.

5

CLASSROOM TRADITIONS

Herb hopped off the school bus at his brand-new bus stop, which was just down the block from Great Aunt Lucinda's mansion. It had taken a few days for him to get used to a new route home and to feel confident about where, exactly, he was supposed to get off the bus. But now that Herb was partway through the first week of third grade, he was feeling pretty good about his new routine. That didn't mean he was feeling good about his family's new *house* . . . just the routine.

Herb still didn't like that they'd had to move, and he still thought Great Aunt Lucinda's house was creepy. He'd loved his family's old house, and he missed it. He wished he could go back, to visit at least, but with those college kids living there now, it wasn't his anymore. Surprisingly, Herb also missed sharing a room with his big brother. But one thing that took the sting out of this move was the fact that school had started— at least Herb had something good to look forward to every day.

Like his big sister, Herb loved school. In fact, he loved school so much that he did *extra* math at the university where Dad worked (Freddy called this Herb's "Tiny Genius" math class). With Dad now back at work—classes at the college had started this week, too—and Herb and his siblings back in school, things were as close to normal as they had been in a long time.

Except that for the Peaches, *normal* now meant living in a mansion.

That was not normal. Who lived in a mansion? None of Herb's school friends, that was for sure. Only people in movies lived in mansions. Rich people. The Peaches had never been rich, and they were *still* not rich.

But actually, Herb had realized, they kind of *had* been millionaires . . . for a little while, anyway. Now they were more like ten-percent-millionaires. Herb had tried to explain his family's strange story when it was his turn to speak in sharing circle that day. "When my mom was still alive," he'd explained to his new classmates, "she worked as an inventor. Mom didn't make very much money doing that because no one really liked any of her stuff, and also, some of it didn't really turn out right or work the way it was supposed to. But before she died, Mom was working on these special things called solar clings. They're these neat stickers that people can put on windows in their house, and they help collect energy from the sun—"

His teacher, Mr. Andrus, had cut in. "Do these solar clings work like solar *panels* on a roof?" he asked. "Or windmills? Those are both things that collect energy, and help to power things." Mr. Andrus pulled up some pictures of solar panels and windmills on the smart board to show the rest of the class what he was talking about.

"Yes," Herb said. "But Mom's solar window clings are smaller. And they're stickers. And they're pretty, because they look like art. Solar panels are kind of ugly and boring."

"Gotcha," Mr. Andrus said with a grin. He nodded for Herb to continue.

"So anyway, this big company wanted to buy Mom's solar clings and they paid her more than a million dollars for them. But she's not alive anymore, so the money went to Dad. Since it wasn't his invention and it's not his money, Dad decided to donate almost all of it to cancer research and he saved some for me and Lucy and Freddy's college. He kept a little bit for fun stuff, but not very much." Herb's classmates had stared at him, and Herb couldn't tell if they were following along with the story. "So we're not *actually* millionaires," Herb had explained. "Not anymore, anyway. But we moved into a fancy rich-person house that my Great Aunt Lucinda gave us. Oh, and we also got to keep her four dogs and we're opening a bed-and-breakfast."

"You've had quite the summer," Mr. Andrus said. Herb wasn't sure why, but he kind of got the feeling that Mr. Andrus thought he was fibbing. When his new teacher got to know him, hopefully he would realize Herb almost always told the truth.

Herb opened his mouth to speak again, eager to tell his classmates about the baby mice he'd adopted that summer, and about the Peach Pie Truck, and the beach house they'd stayed at in North Carolina, and the Ohio

Food Truck Festival. But before he could get any more words out, Mr. Andrus cut him off again to let another kid have a turn.

As soon as Herb got home from school that day, he called out for his big sister. "Lucy!"

No answer.

"Luuuuuuu-cy!" he tried again. Rudy the dog came careening around the corner and scratched at Herb's leg.

When Lucy still didn't answer, Herb hopped across the kitchen and pressed the fourth-floor button on the old-fashioned intercom. "Lucy!" he shrieked into it.

When he *still* didn't get any answer, Herb pressed the second-floor intercom button, then the third-floor, then the fourth-floor again. The only response he got was from Freddy, who shouted back through the little speaker, "You don't have to scream into the intercom, Herb!"

Freddy was allowed to bike to and from school and had somehow been getting home before Herb's bus dropped him off every day. It was kind of annoying that Herb was always the last Peach kid home. But it was also nice, since it meant he never had to be in Great Aunt Lucinda's haunted house alone. It was always different before, when he'd come by to visit their great aunt's house as a guest. But now, the scary noises were *his* scary noises, and Herb couldn't pop in the car and ride away from them at the end of the night.

So even though he hated getting home last most days, Herb wasn't sure he'd *ever* want to be alone in this house. He was maybe starting to get used to some of the strange noises the house made (and Lucy had promised him Great Aunt Lucinda had been joking about the ghosts), but this didn't make him any less creeped out. Some of Herb's friends thought living in a mansion sounded really cool, but he'd come to realize it was actually very strange and kind of lonely.

Eager to talk to his sister (who was Herb's very best friend and favorite person in the whole wide world), Herb raced up the wide staircase to the fourth floor. All four of the dogs raced after him. If it weren't for the dogs, Herb would truly hate living in the mansion—but the addition of Great Aunt Lucinda's four dogs made this whole situation a whole lot better. They were a lot of work, and Herb had to clean up a lot of messes that they made, but the work was worth it. The pack followed Herb almost everywhere he went, so he was almost never actually alone.

By the time he reached the very tip-top fourth floor of the house (the little half story that he and Lucy shared, just the two of them), Herb was out of breath and panting. He raced into Lucy's room, but found it empty. Herb leaned over and put his hands on his knees, trying to catch his breath. When he stood back up, his sister had appeared, as if by magic.

Herb's mouth popped open. "Where did you come from?" he asked.

Lucy glanced at her closet. Herb thought she looked a little guilty about something. She asked, "What do you mean?"

"I mean," Herb said, "you weren't here a second ago, but now you are." Great Aunt Lucinda's house was enormous, which made it hard for Herb to find people sometimes. But he was pretty sure Lucy must have been hiding from him somewhere, since he was almost positive she hadn't been in her room when he first walked in.

Lucy laughed, but didn't answer his question. Instead, she said, "How was your third day at school?" All four dogs hopped up onto Lucy's bed, bouncing off the floor at almost the same time, reminding Herb of four little popped kernels of popcorn. Herb tumbled down on the floor, and they all immediately jumped back down again to nuzzle up beside him. Vix nosed her snout into Herb's pocket, trying to snag a treat. Herb had been working on starting to teach the four dogs some manners and basic tricks, which meant he almost always had some fake-bacon treats tucked into his pocket. Herb was hoping that if the pack learned to be a little better behaved, he could take them to Birch Pond retirement community to visit Aunt Lucinda. But they had a *lot* of work to do before that could happen.

"My day was okay," Herb said. He pointed at Rudolph, who usually went by Rudy. "Rudy, sit!"

Rather than sitting, Rudy dashed across the room and dragged Lucy's T-shirt out from under her desk chair. He whipped his head from side to side, tossing the shirt around like a rag doll.

"Drop it!" Herb ordered. Rudy raced out of the room, set the T-shirt just outside the door, then turned and barked to signal that he was ready to play a game of chase.

"Not a great day?" Lucy asked, swiping Vix—short for Vixen—off the floor and cuddling her into her lap. Herb thought it was funny that Aunt Lucinda had named all four of her dogs after Santa's reindeer. Their great aunt *loved* old Christmas movies and always enjoyed getting her house all dressed up for the holidays. She'd told Herb that having Santa's reindeer as pets helped her keep the holiday spirit alive all year long.

Herb scrambled over to retrieve the stolen T-shirt, then sat down on Lucy's bedroom floor and proceeded to put Rudy *in* the shirt. All the dogs seemed to like wearing human clothes; at the very least, they all tolerated it. And they all looked very cute in little costumes. "No, it was a pretty good day," Herb said. "I really like Mr. Andrus. Today he told us about some of the special events he does during the year in his classroom. Once every month, he has this thing called Books for Breakfast where we all read the same book and then we get to come to school early one morning and eat muffins and talk about the book together—like a book club. Sometimes, he even invites the author to come and talk to us from his computer!"

"Wow!" Lucy said. "That sounds amazing, Herb."

"The first book he picked for us to read is called *Meet Yasmin!* about a girl named Yasmin and it looks really good. It's not very long." Herb was excited about his teacher's morning book club. He and Lucy had sort of done a book club that summer in the food truck, but it wasn't quite the same as talking about a book with his teacher and friends. "Also, he started something called The Tournament of Books. He's going to read us a picture book every single day this fall, and then we all get to vote for the books we like the best until we figure out the all-time class favorite."

"I wish I'd had that guy as my teacher in third

grade," Lucy muttered. "That all sounds so fun!" She wrapped her hand around Vix's mouth, since the little pup was now trying to chew and de-stuff Lucy's stuffed duck. Lucy slept with the duck most nights, but was always willing to share it with Herb when he was feeling sad or lonely or scared. He'd borrowed the duck every single night since they'd moved into the mansion; it was strange sleeping in a room without Freddy's deep breathing thundering out of the bunk above him.

"Yeah," Herb said. "My teacher is pretty great so far . . ." He trailed off. The thing he *hadn't* told Lucy about was the special Mother-Son Tea his teacher hosted each year the week before Thanksgiving break. It was a chance for all the boys in the room to bring their moms in and serve them at a fancy tea party. Mr. Andrus also hosted a Father-Daughter Sharing Feast for the girls in class, so they could invite their dads in for a special afternoon eating snacks together in the classroom.

The problem was, Herb didn't *have* a mother anymore, and he felt weird going to the sharing feast with all the girls and dads . . . so what, exactly, was a guy like him supposed to do?

WHAT CAN YOU GROW OUT OF A PEACH PIT?

FREDDY'S TREEHOUSE
"Nature Room"

The attic
(for storing food)

Freddy's
Woodland
Shack

6

BUILDING PLANS

"Blug blid bluh blubber blumber blay," Freddy announced through a mouthful of food at dinner on Friday night.

"Seriously?" Lucy snapped, glaring at him. "Can you maybe *chew* before you start talking?"

Freddy opened his mouth and chewed in a giant, exaggerated way—like a cow chomping its cud. Then he swallowed and blurted out, "What did the other plumber say? And the carpenter lady?"

Walter Peach took a sip of his sparkling water and delicately wiped his mouth with a cloth napkin Lucy had found in one of the built-in drawers in the mansion's dining room. Freddy found the fussy napkins at Aunt Lucinda's mansion icky and scratchy; they had always been more of a paper towel kind of family (or if it were up to him, Freddy would prefer to just wipe his dirty hands on his pants—that's what pants are *there* for).

"Well," Dad began. "We have some issues."

"Is it the broken faucet in the third-floor guest bathroom?" Herb asked.

"Or the leaky kitchen sink?" Lucy suggested.

"The busted window in my room?" Freddy suggested. He thought it was kinda cool, the way the wind sort of whistled through the cracks in his windowpanes. But he guessed it would be less fun when winter came, and each whistle would bring with it a gust of icy air. "The one that's patched up with duct tape, or the other one that sort of rattles when it's windy?"

"That gross rotted siding above the front porch?" Lucy added. "It's starting to shed off the side of the house in chunks, like lizard skin."

"That's called molting. Some lizards eat their old skin after it flakes off!" Freddy said with a nod. "Did you guys know that lizards can break off a chunk of their own tail if it gets caught by a predator?"

"Are they worried about the peeling paint around all the windows outside?" Herb guessed, ignoring Freddy's very interesting fun fact.

"Have they seen the patch that looks like a wet pee spot on the ceiling below the second-floor guest bathroom?" Freddy asked. "I bet that's not good."

Dad cringed. "Yeah, pretty much."

"Which one?" Lucy asked.

"All of those things and a whole lot more," Dad said, sighing. "Have I even told you kids that the water in the shower in my bathroom and two of the guest bedrooms comes out sort of brown? Fixing plumbing issues in this house is pretty much going to use up all of our fun money, and possibly more. There's no way we're going to have this place ready for guests by Thanksgiving."

Freddy shoved some more noodles in his mouth and said, "Don chay dat."

"Yeah, Dad," Herb agreed. "Don't say that."

"I'm just being realistic," Dad said, shaking his head. "I know Lucinda is expecting us to have things up and running here in a matter of months, but I can't see how that's possible. We're going to need to do a lot of the work on this house ourselves in order to afford every- thing. We can handle some of the painting, and the littler projects, but frankly, I don't know as much as I'd like to know about plumbing and carpentry work."

"Do you know *anything* about carpentry or plumbing work?" Lucy asked slowly.

"I've read a few books and watched some of those home improvement shows on TV," Dad said. "I'm sure we can figure out enough to handle some of the basics.

That will help cut costs, but it's going to take time. And a lot of hard work."

Freddy and his siblings exchanged a look. Their dad was not the kind of guy who should touch any plumbing pipes, or even so much as *pick up* a hammer and nails or electric drill, but how were they supposed to explain that to him? Dad was definitely a smart, capable guy . . . when it came to bookish stuff and futzing with his soil samples in the lab. When it came to practical stuff like building or repairing things (or even making dinner), he'd never really been a genius. *Mom* had always been the one who handled home repairs and assembled any furniture that needed building; after she died, Dad had hired people whenever they needed things done that couldn't be ignored or put off indefinitely.

But if Freddy had learned anything during their Great Peach Experiment in the food truck, it was that their dad was actually somewhat willing to adjust and learn when he had no other choice—so maybe if Dad *said* he could take on some of the repairs himself, it was their job to believe in him and support his efforts. "I'm happy to help out," Freddy offered. "I do a lot of the building at Cardboard Camp, so I at least know how to work a hammer."

"That's good," Dad said. "Hammers have never been something I've ever really gotten the hang of."

Again, the kids exchanged nervous looks.

"The place doesn't need to be *perfect* by Thanksgiving," Freddy pointed out. "We might not ever be some kind of luxury hotel, but the Peach Pit has charm. We've got that going for us."

"True," Dad agreed.

"I think we should make a to-do list so we can tick things off as we finish them, and so we have some idea of what's left to get done," Lucy suggested.

"Maybe we should make one list for house stuff and another that has all the things we need to do for the bed-and-breakfast," Herb added.

"Yes," Dad agreed. "That's an excellent plan."

Lucy reached across the table and grabbed Freddy's sketchbook, which was sitting beside his dinner plate. She opened it up to the back and ripped out a fresh, clean piece of paper. As the family rattled off ideas, Lucy took notes:

TO-DO LIST: The Peach Pit

1. Hire a plumber
   To do: lots of broken faucets, pee-stain leak under second-floor bathroom tub, kitchen sink, brown water in showers
2. Fix broken door handles and stair rail banisters
3. Paint trim around the windows outside
4. Fix/repair those sections of lizard-skin siding
5. Peel off living room wallpaper and paint
6. Paint and repair guest room walls
7. Clean and paint dining room
8. Replace cracked windows

HOW TO OPEN A B&B

1. Plan & buy stuff to put in guest rooms
    Shampoo, Conditioner, Robes??, Bedding,
    Pillows, Slippers?, New art?
2. Organize and rearrange and clean guest room
   furniture
3. Clean guest bathrooms (after plumber is gone)
4. Figure out how to take reservations, check
   guests in when they show up, collect money,
   buy breakfast supplies, do permit and business
   research, and other important details like
   that
    ** Hire our B&B host to help figure all this
       stuff out!! <- I'm on it!
5. Name the B&B   <- What's wrong with
6. Mop floors & wash windows   The Peach Pit?!
7. Figure out what we're going to offer guests
   for breakfast (since we have to offer the
   second B part of the B&B, not just a bed)
8. Practice serving breakfast

Lucy tucked the pen in her mouth and chewed on the cap. "Can anyone think of anything else right now?" she asked.

"It's a good thing this house is on the Historic Register," Freddy pointed out. "Since it means we can't knock down any walls or anything. We're kind of stuck with what we got, and even that's more than we can handle."

Dad rested his elbows on the table and leaned his forehead into his open palms. "It's too much," he said. "I wonder if we should just let Lucinda sell the place, and we can go back home where we at least *know* about everything that's wrong with the house."

"Nuh-uh," Freddy protested. He refused to go back to sharing a room with Herb now that he knew what a luxury it was to have his own private bedroom. Also, he'd convinced Dad to let him turn the old shed in the backyard into his personal art studio. And he was excited to help with some of the house repair projects; he'd had plenty of experience helping build stuff at Cardboard Camp, and he could use that knowledge to help with the Peach Pit! Freddy *loved* living in a mansion, and he couldn't *wait* to turn this Experiment into another successful business.

"I'm not ready to leave," Herb declared, which surprised Freddy a bit. He couldn't tell if his little brother liked living in the mansion, or if he kind of didn't. "I want to keep my dogs. If we go home, where would they live?"

Dad considered this. Their little house on the other side of town just barely had room for three kids, let alone three kids *and* four dogs. Also, they didn't have a fenced yard the pups could play in. Here at the mansion, there was a big nature preserve filled with wildflowers and giant trees out back. Freddy and his siblings had decided it almost felt like they lived in a private park or something. (Also, because of the size of their new house and the giant grounds, Freddy's friends had taken to calling him Prince Freddy ever since the family had moved in.)

"I don't know what to say about the dogs, Herb," Dad said.

"I don't want to move out of Aunt Lucinda's mansion, either," Lucy blurted out. "I love my room, and I'm excited to fill this place with guests. I can't wait to tell them about all the cool stuff we have in Duluth. I think running a B and B will be great! One of the books I read this summer, *Front Desk*, is about a girl whose family kind of operates this little motel, and she takes care of the front desk, and it just seems like it would be fun to meet a bunch of people from other states and cities and stuff."

"You sound just like your mother," Dad said. This

comment made Freddy blush, even though his dad was talking about Lucy and not him. When people talked about his mom, it always made Freddy feel uncomfortable and sort of squirmy.

"I *can't* leave," Freddy announced, trying to shift the topic away from Mom. "I already started a new, huge, important project out in my art shed." The only good thing that had happened at school that week was a conversation Freddy had had with his art teacher. Usually, when teachers called him in for a special conversation, Freddy guessed he was in trouble or that they were going to tell him he needed to get extra help with his work. But when his *art* teacher called him in for a meeting, it was usually a good thing. "Mrs. Fig told me about this citywide art competition that's happening this fall, and she asked me if I'd be willing to represent our school in the show. They award prizes for the winning pieces, and there's going to be a gallery where they display the artists' work and everything."

"Freddy!" Dad exclaimed. "That's incredible. Good for you."

"Thanks," Freddy said, his face flushing pinker. "It's pretty cool. You have to be nominated by a teacher." Freddy was very excited to have been chosen by his art teacher, but he was even more excited to figure out exactly what he was going to enter in the show. He guessed a lot of people would submit paintings or clay sculptures or drawings. Much as he liked sketching, none of those mediums were really Freddy's style.

What he'd decided he *really* wanted to do for the competition was design and build a miniature replica of his dream treehouse. This was a project he'd been planning and thinking about for years, and he'd even been sketching up some sample rooms in his sketchbook. After spending the past week building at Cardboard Camp, and looking ahead to the next few months getting inspired by all the fun construction at home, it seemed like the perfect time to focus on a fun building project. He just hadn't yet decided on the exact design or figured out what he might construct it out of—cardboard? Recycled cans? Sugar cubes? Wood? He also had to think about how he could make a case for how this specific project represented *him* and his artistic style.

He'd kind of bent the truth when he told his dad he had to stay at the mansion because he'd already started the piece. The truth was, he hadn't *actually* started building it yet, but his blueprints and designs and idea-sketches were scattered all over his new art shed, and Freddy was looking forward to using his very own private space to work on whatever it was he might end up building for the competition. For the first time in his life, Freddy had a space that made him feel like a real artist.

"Well, it sure sounds like you all want to stay," Dad said. "And I certainly do love this house and all the memories in it. I guess I don't really want to see it passed into the hands of some stranger." He gestured for Lucy to hand over their to-do lists and said, "So let's take a look at these lists and figure out how we're going to get it all done."

TO-DO LIST: The Peach Pit

1. Hire a plumber
   To do: lots of broken faucets, pee-stain leak under second-floor bathroom tub, kitchen sink, brown water in showers
2. Fix broken door handles and stair rail banisters
3. Paint trim around the windows outside
4. Fix/repair those sections of lizard-skin siding
5. Peel off living room wallpaper and paint
6. Paint and repair guest room walls
7. Clean and paint dining room
8. Replace cracked windows

HOW TO OPEN A B&B

1. Plan & buy stuff to put in guest rooms
   Shampoo, Conditioner, Robes??, Bedding,
   Pillows, Slippers?, New art?
2. Organize and rearrange and clean guest room
   furniture
3. Clean guest bathrooms (after plumber is gone)
4. Figure out how to take reservations, check
   guests in when they show up, collect money,
   buy breakfast supplies, and other important
   details like that
   ** Hire our B&B host to help figure all this
   stuff out!! <- **I'm on it!**
5. Name the B&B   <- **What's wrong with**
6. Mop floors & wash windows   **The Peach Pit?!**
7. Figure out what we're going to offer guests
   for breakfast (since we have to offer the
   second B part of the B&B, not just a bed)
8. Practice serving breakfast
9. ~~Get tuxedoes so we can pretend to be~~
   ~~butlers and act like we're working at a~~
   ~~castle~~ ← NO!

7

DIGGING THROUGH THE PAST

That weekend, the Peaches finally began taking some of the first baby steps to fix up Great Aunt Lucinda's mansion. There were a lot of obvious things that needed care and attention, but Lucy had quickly volunteered for the job she thought looked the most fun: peeling all the old wallpaper off the living room walls.

First, she took all the creepy paintings off the walls (Herb had begged her to move the portraits out to the garage while they worked on the room, since he was convinced the people in the paintings would come to life and haunt them at night if they were left stacked up inside). Once all the old wallpaper was gone, they would get to paint the room a soothing color, and possibly hang some new art. Dad thought the old portraits gave the room character and reflected the history of the house, but Lucy kind of agreed with Herb: The people in the portraits had a spooky, lifelike quality and she wasn't sad to see them gone.

The wallpaper in the giant living room was dark green with faded maroon flowers, and peeling it off the walls was incredibly satisfying. Using her fingernail (or sometimes, when it was really stuck, the edge of a metal pancake spatula), she would gently pry up one corner of the paper to loosen it from the wall. If she tugged the paper just so—nice and slow—she could usually get a long strip to peel away from the wall cleanly. Sometimes, little bits of the paper would stick to the wall—that's when Herb would swoop in and scratch at the leftover sticky bits with a tiny scraper. The two of them made a great team.

While they worked, Lucy put on audio books or music to keep herself and Herb entertained. Whenever he wasn't scraping bits off the wall, Herb spent time working on training the dogs. All four of the pups were finally getting to be so-so at the "Sit" command, but none of them could figure out what "Drop it," or "Off," or "No" meant. They loved stealing (and chewing) things that didn't belong to them—socks, stuffed animals, sneakers—and they were constantly jumping up on people and furniture. They ran away every time

Herb tried to put any one of them in a collar or leash, but they seemed perfectly willing to wear adorable little dog clothes.

After living with Dasher, Donny, Vix, and Rudy for a week, Lucy had discovered the four dogs had absolutely no manners and were much more fun to *visit* than they were to live with. She was glad Herb had taken on all the doggie duties, since *someone* had to keep the four fluffy pups in line and Lucy got far too frustrated far too quickly. Earlier in the week, Aunt Lucinda had told Lucy how much she missed her "little darlings," and she'd already been begging the Peach kids to bring them by for a visit. Lucy hoped (but kind of doubted) her little brother would whip them into shape soon.

"Lucy?" Herb said, clicking off the audio book of *The Penderwicks on Gardam Street*. It was a sequel to the first *Penderwicks* book, which the Peaches had read aloud together during their summer road trip.

"Mm-hmm," Lucy replied, carefully picking at a piece of wallpaper that really didn't want to be separated from the wall it had been covering for more than half a century.

"I don't think it's fair that you and Freddy each get your own room to decorate for the bed-and-breakfast, and I have to share with Dad."

Lucy had been waiting for Herb to bring this up. The previous night, after dinner, they had sat down as a family and figured out how they would divide up some of the tasks that needed to get done around the house. They would all pitch in to help with some stuff—painting the outside window trim and inside rooms, fixing "simple" stuff like doorknobs, and other little repairs that didn't need a professional eye.

After Dad told Freddy he couldn't take a "school break" to help with all the construction projects and getting the business up and running, Freddy had turned on the charm to ask for something else. He'd *begged* their dad to let him take ownership of cleaning up and decorating one of the guest rooms. He had done some research and found that a lot of other bed-and-breakfasts decorated each of their guest rooms in a unique style to make every room feel special and one-of-a-kind. Freddy wanted to have a chance to design one of their guest rooms in his own way, and promised he would make it tasteful. Lucy thought this was an excellent idea, and asked to have a guest room of *her* own to plan and fix up, too. Dad agreed, then said he and Herb could work together to figure out the plans for the third and final guest room. They agreed to each use $1,000 of the money they'd won at the Food Truck Festival that summer to purchase bedding and decorations, and the deal was that Dad had to approve each big purchase.

Herb had immediately set his mouth in a firm, grumpy line and announced, "That's not fair!" But Dad had shushed him and moved on to the next matter. Now, almost twenty-four hours later, Herb was wearing the same peeved expression again. "I want to decide what the third guest room is going to look like, all by myself," he declared. "Sharing with Dad is poopy."

"I'm sure Dad will let you do most of the planning for the room you guys are working on together," Lucy said. "He just wants to oversee things, since . . ." She trailed off, because Herb didn't like to be reminded of this fact. ". . . since you're only eight, Herb."

"But I'm more mature than Freddy is," Herb argued. "And he gets to design a guest room all by himself!"

This was quite true, Lucy thought to herself. Herb was extremely mature; Freddy not as much. But Freddy had an artistic eye, so this kind of project was perfect for him. She thought her dad had made the right choice in how he assigned responsibility for the guest rooms. "You can help me pick out stuff to decorate my guest room," Lucy promised. "I decided I'm going to turn mine into a Winter Wonderland! Since Great Aunt Lucinda likes Christmas so much, I think she'll think that's fun." Lucy also happened to know, from her one quick peek up into the giant attic space, that there were wintery decorations *galore* tucked away up there. "I don't want to make it *Christmas* themed, because then if someone who doesn't celebrate Christmas stays there, they might feel uncomfortable. But I thought a winter wonderland design would be really fun, and it suits our Northern Minnesota setting."

"A touch of winter, even in summer." Herb grinned. "I love that idea."

For a while, Lucy and Herb talked about what Lucy's guest room might look like. Then Herb told Lucy he wanted to make the room he and Dad were responsible for *fruit* themed. "Because we're the Peaches!" Herb explained. "Also, I've noticed Great Aunt Lucinda had a lot of pretty fruit art hanging around the house, so she must like it and she'll probably think it's super fun since it's also our last name."

Lucy laughed. "That's so cute, Herbie."

"And I was also thinking," Herb went on, "that we could maybe hang some of Mom's solar window clings in the windows of each of the guest rooms. One of the designs had little peaches on it, and that would be perfect for the fruit room. If we use her solar clings, it would help us save money on electricity and it would kind of be like Mom is helping."

Lucy climbed down from the step stool she'd been working on and gave her brother a big hug. "That's the perfect way to include her."

By late Saturday afternoon, Lucy decided they needed a break from the living room wallpaper-peeling. So Herb trotted out to the back to run around in the nature preserve with his pack. On the second floor, Freddy was happily watching YouTube instructional videos, while futzing around to try to reattach and repair some of the broken doorknobs throughout the house. Meanwhile, Dad was swimming in a mess of pipes he'd pulled out from under the sink in a second-floor bathroom. (Based on the fact that Dad kept yelling out, "Experiment fail! Start again from step one!" over and over, he was going to be tied up in there for a while.)

So with her family all busy, Lucy finally had some time to sneak up into the attic. Ever since she'd found the magnificent hidden room at the top of the house earlier that week, Lucy had been trying to find an opportunity to crawl up there and get a good look around. She'd raced home from school every day, but timing had never worked out quite right. One day there was an electrician poking around up on the fourth floor, another day her dad had asked her to bike over to the grocery store for milk and eggs and choose something for dinner, and on Thursday she'd had an essay to write for Language Arts (her first of the year, so she wanted to make it good!).

But now, finally, she could close her bedroom door and explore the bonus room hidden above her closet. Lucy climbed up on the ledge in her giant closet and pushed open the small door nestled into the ceiling. It took some wriggling and a lot of arm muscles, but after some awkward stumbles and a few loud grunts, she was able to pull herself up into the dusty attic space. Once inside, she realized the space was even bigger than she'd originally dared to hope; at least as big as the hallway, her bedroom, and Herb's bedroom combined. The old wood planks stretching across the floor were wide and bumpy, and the ceiling was slanted and peaked like the roof overhead, which made the space look extra cozy and nook-like. There weren't any lamps or lightbulbs, but there was enough dusty daylight coming in from the cracked windows at each end of the house that Lucy could see pretty well.

It was stale and stuffy in the closed-up space, but she didn't care. Lucy wiped a trail of sweat off her forehead and stepped gingerly across the room, hoping the boards under her feet wouldn't collapse. She was eager to explore all the boxes and storage bins that lined the walls. There were several clear plastic bins filled with Christmas decorations—lights, fake greenery, tree decorations, a whole bushel of fake plastic grapes coated in glitter, and even a giant container of wrapping paper and silvery bows. She peeked into one of the cardboard boxes nearby; it was stuffed with probably every holiday card Great Aunt Lucinda had ever received in her entire life.

She scooched along to the next area of the attic, which was piled high with broken wicker end tables, a dusty three-legged upholstered foot stool, and some mismatched wooden furniture that had very likely been around since the house was first built in the early 1900s.

Moving along to the next pile, she found a trunk filled with old bedsheets, curtains, and other musty, stained cloth stuff. The inside of the trunk smelled funny, so Lucy quickly flipped it closed again.

There were boxes upon boxes of photographs, photo albums, and one that had a dozen or so creepy old dolls. She would definitely not tell Herb about that box. Over the years, Freddy had told her and Herb dozens of horrifying "true" stories about dolls that had come to life and eaten or swapped bodies with or otherwise tortured their owners. Lucy really wished *she* didn't know all these creepy dolls were here, sitting in the space above her bed, possibly angry about being cooped up inside a musty old box. What if they came to life? It happened in books and Freddy's stories, so that wasn't totally out of the question.

After sealing up the box of dolls, Lucy returned to the photo albums. The first one she opened was filled with pictures of Aunt Lucinda as a much younger woman. There were little kids in some of the pictures, and on closer inspection, Lucy felt fairly sure that one of the boys in the photos was her dad! She flipped through the album. The pictures took her from an ice cream shop on a boardwalk near the ocean; to one of Duluth's many creeks; to the sandy peninsula sticking off one end of her hometown, called Park Point. It was fun looking at old pictures of her dad, probably from when he was about her age.

Pushing aside a pile of crumbling boxes of vases and fake flowers, Lucy found a gorgeous, huge, old-fashioned dollhouse tucked under one of the attic eaves. She dragged it forward for a closer look. The dollhouse was an almost-exact replica of the Peach Pit! There were a bunch of fruit paintings on the walls inside the dollhouse—paintings that matched some of the art Lucy had just recently taken down from walls around the house!—and a few pieces of broken miniature furniture were tossed about inside the rooms of the house. But other than that, the giant playhouse was empty. Lucy pushed it to the center of the attic, planning to bring it downstairs to share with Herb just as soon as she could get it out of here. He'd love it, and it would be the perfect place for her little brother to display some of his most prized collections.

Herb needed a little treasure of his very own, and Lucy was glad she could be the one to give him something special to smile about. Even if he didn't get his very own room to decorate, now he'd have a whole *house* to spruce up, all by himself. Lucy startled at the sound of Freddy's thundering footsteps pounding up the stairs beneath her. She scrambled over to the little attic door, slid through the narrow opening, and dropped back down into her closet. Heart pounding, she pulled the door to her closet closed before her brothers spotted the trapdoor to Lucy's secret world.

FREDDY'S FAMOUS
BLUEBERRY BUTTERMILK PANCAKES

- 2 eggs
- 2 C buttermilk
- 1/4 C vegetable oil
- 1 1/4 C flour
- 2 T sugar
- 2 t baking powder
- 1 t baking soda
- 1/2 t salt
- 1 C fresh or frozen, thawed blueberries (not sweetened!)

Heat griddle to 400° F. Beat eggs, buttermilk, and oil together. Add flour, sugar, baking powder, baking soda, and salt. Stir gently until the lumps are gone. Blend in the blueberries (sometimes it turns the batter blue!). Scoop out about 1/4 cup of batter and cook pancakes on the griddle or pan until bubbles form and the edges of the pancake start to look dry. Turn and cook on the other side.

8

A JOB FOR HERB

As he walked toward the glass double doors leading into Aunt Lucinda's senior living complex for a visit, Herb realized he was still feeling a little grumpy with his great aunt. If *she* hadn't decided it was time for her to move out of her mansion, and if *she* hadn't wanted to "keep it in the family," and if *she* hadn't made the crazy decision to give the house to Herb and his family, then *he* wouldn't have had to move out of his old, snuggly, comfortable house and live in a real-life *haunted* house. Sure, having the dogs to care for was nice. And fine, Herb was maybe starting to get used to some of the noises the rickety mansion made. But most of the time, his aunt's old, creepy house still felt too big, too echo-y, and too spooky to him.

Also, living in an old house—especially one that

needed a lot of fixing and patching and painting—was a lot of work! Herb had pale pink and cream paint on all ten fingers, wallpaper glue trapped under his nails, and a stubborn black Sharpie line across the left side of his face (the line was Freddy's fault, from the afternoon Herb had helped him measure some scraps of wood out in his art shed). Herb was good at many things, but it turned out mansion renovation was not one of them.

Herb and his family had spent almost all their free time the past few weeks doing all kinds of boring stuff like painting walls, scrubbing sinks, and taking apart faucets. The faucet project had started out fun, since Herb liked seeing stuff pulled apart to try to learn how it worked . . . but it hadn't *ended* fun, since Dad couldn't figure out how to get the sink parts all back together. Once they turned the water on again, the faucet had shot streams of water into the air like a fancy fountain at a park. Their mansion really was a pit—the Peach Pit, as Freddy lovingly called it—and they had a lot to do before guests could come to stay.

Their family had spent a lot of time since moving into the mansion researching all the legal stuff and permits and things they would need for a B&B and their construction project. And after breaking more stuff than he had actually tried to fix, Dad finally caved and hired the daughter of one of his coworkers at the university to manage and oversee the construction. Dad kept insisting on "helping" with all the work—plumbing, building, and even electrical projects—but Herb could see that Dad was better at microscopes and data spreadsheets than he was at circuit breakers and nail guns.

Herb pulled open the giant front doors of the senior living center and greeted the front desk guy. "Hey, Bernie!"

Bernie waved back. "Herb, my man," he said, holding up a hand for a high five. "How've you been?"

"Pretty good," Herb replied. "What's on the group schedule right now?"

"You made it for Bingo," Bernie said, nodding. "Good timing."

Good timing, indeed. Herb *loved* Bingo. He actually loved most things about Great Aunt Lucinda's senior living center, and after visiting her there a handful of times, it was easy to see why she'd decided to move out of her big, lonely house. Every day there were activities galore—Bingo, card tournaments, art lessons, music time, dance parties, movie night, and (Herb's personal favorite) afternoon tea-and-scones socials. Lots of Great Aunt Lucinda's friends lived in other apartments in the facility, and she'd already made a whole bunch of new friends. The staff was always really friendly, and Herb had quickly discovered he was *very* popular with everyone at Birch Pond. He felt like a superstar when he came by to visit. Luckily, the mansion was less than a mile from Birch Pond, and Dad let Herb bike there all by himself as long as he promised to stick to the paved bike path that ran alongside London Road, and only crossed the street at stoplights.

"Can I go in?" Herb asked Bernie.

"For sure," Bernie said, flashing him a smile. "Win big."

Just as Herb was heading through the inner doors to the lounge where the Bingo games were always held, he noticed some of the plants in the lobby were looking a little wilty. He poked his finger into the dirt and found them dry as an overcooked pie crust. "Is it okay if I water these?" Herb asked Bernie.

"Be my guest," Bernie said with a gravelly laugh.

Herb grabbed a plastic cup from the kitchen and spent a few minutes tending to all the plants in the lobby. Some of the plants had a few dead leaves, which he removed. Herb noticed that the Christmas cactus was almost in bloom, even though they were still a few months from Christmas. Herb remembered that his mom had loved her Christmas cactus, in part because it *never* bloomed at Christmas—sometimes, it actually bloomed in the spring, which Mom had always found absolutely hilarious.

As Herb wrapped up his rounds, Bernie called out, "Want to feed the fish and the turtles, too?"

Herb whipped around. "Can I?"

"Not my favorite job," Bernie admitted.

"Yeah, I want to do it," Herb said, bouncing on his toes. Bernie showed him how much of each kind of food to give the animals, and then taught him how to use a little device to test the water in the tank. Herb loved taking care of living things. That summer, Dad had let him keep and care for three little mouse babies during their food truck road trip (but he'd released them when it was clear they would be happier back in the wild). When they'd returned from their trip, he had planned to ask Dad for a hamster or rabbit or hedgehog of his very own, but he'd gotten Aunt Lucinda's four mischievous dogs instead (which was *much* better than he ever would have dared hoped for).

By the time Herb had finished his jobs, the Bingo game was just wrapping up—so there would be no prizes for Herb that day. But that was okay; getting to water the plants and feed the Birch Pond pets was even better! He headed into the lounge and joined Great Aunt Lucinda and a few of her friends—Joye, Caroline, and Diane—at one of the tables near the door. Today, Herb immediately noticed, Great Aunt Lucinda was wearing Herb's favorite wig of all: a very flattering silver wig that curled all around her face and made her look friendly, squishy, and extra grandmother-y. Some days, depending on what matched her mood and outfit for the day, Aunt Lucinda wore her silly wigs—pink, jet-black, spiky blond—and they made Herb feel a little uncomfortable. The worst was the wig Freddy called "The Spaghetti Bowl," since it looked like pieces of cooked spaghetti draped on top of Great Aunt Lucinda's head.

Caroline, Diane, and Aunt Lucinda hugged him and planted kisses on his cheeks (Joye wasn't much of a hugger . . . or a smiler). Then all four of the women listened eagerly as Herb told them stories about the dogs' naughty behavior from the past few days.

"Dasher got up on one of the dining room chairs and ate Freddy's entire bagel yesterday morning before school," he said, laughing at the memory of the tiny dog sitting at the table, eating off a plate like some kind of invited guest. "And Vix likes to lick her butt while she lays on Dad's pillow."

Great Aunt Lucinda and her friends all hooted with laughter.

"When will you be able to bring them down to visit

me?" Aunt Lucinda asked. She knew Herb was working hard on training them to behave on a leash and be able to act like proper dogs when they were in public . . . but she also knew it was a big job. The pups had spent the first few years of their lives living with pretty much no discipline or rules or training at all. Herb had a major task ahead of him. "Since I promised your dad I wouldn't come by the house until it's ready for guests, I need you to bring my little treasures here to see me!"

"I'm working on it," Herb said. "Things aren't going super well."

"With the dogs, or the house?" Aunt Lucinda asked.

"Both," Herb said, cringing.

"Uh-oh." Aunt Lucinda shared a look with her friends.

Suddenly, Herb felt bad for saying that. He knew how much his siblings and Dad loved the mansion, and how hard they were all working to grow the Peach Pit into something nice-ish. He didn't want it to seem like he was tattling on his family with Great Aunt Lucinda. "I mean," he said, searching for better words, "it's just a lot of work. The dogs *and* the house. But things are coming along."

Aunt Lucinda smiled. "I'm happy to hear it."

"It's a good thing I have the dogs to keep me busy," Herb said. "Because there's not much I can really do to help with the B and B."

"Why's that?" Aunt Lucinda's friend Diane asked.

"Well, there are going to be three guest rooms in total," he began. "We decided it would be fun if each room has its own personality, since it seems like that's what a lot of B and B owners do. Anyway, Dad decided it didn't make much sense for all of us to spend time working on all of them, so we're kind of splitting the three guest rooms up and different people are managing different projects in the house."

"Makes sense," Caroline announced. She glanced at Aunt Lucinda and said, "Seems like Walter is figuring stuff out."

Herb shrugged. "Well, then Dad decided that *Lucy* could be in charge of decorating one of the guest rooms." He paused, not wanting to reveal the big secret, that Lucy had decided to turn her guest room into a wintery wonderland. Aunt Lucinda would be so excited when she saw it! "And since he's the second oldest and the most creative and arty of us, Freddy gets to figure out how to decorate one room by himself, too." Herb scowled. Freddy couldn't even decide what he wanted to do with his guest room in the B&B—he just kept sketching ideas, but didn't seem to be making any actual progress toward fixing it up and getting it ready for guests. Lucy was responsible, and it made sense that she got to be in charge of part of this project all by herself; but Freddy wasn't even that much older than Herb, and anyway, he was going to be busy working on his art competition project for the next few months! He didn't deserve to get a guest room of his very own to be in charge of. "But I have to work with *Dad*, and we're going to share the third guest room."

"Ah," Great Aunt Lucinda said. "I can see how that would be frustrating for you."

"It is! I begged Dad to let me be in charge of one of the rooms all by myself, but he said I'm too young and that it would be more fun and easier if we work together." Herb sighed. Since he was the youngest, Dad always assumed he was the least capable of the Peach kids. But he had proven, time and again, just how responsible he was. "I'm good at being in charge of stuff by myself, and I'm very responsible!" Herb huffed. "Today I watered all the plants and fed the fish and the turtles in the lobby. Bernie said I did a great job. And I took care of my mice all summer, and I always finish my homework without anyone reminding me, and—"

"Sounds to me like you need to prove to your dad,

once and for all, just how mature and responsible you are," Aunt Lucinda said.

"How am I supposed to do that?" Herb asked. Then he brightened. "What if I got a job?"

"That's an idea." Great Aunt Lucinda chuckled.

"Do you think they would hire me to work here at Birch Pond?" Herb asked, glancing at the group of ladies sitting around the table.

"Most of the staff here have nursing degrees . . . or they're at least eighteen years old," Aunt Lucinda said. "But—"

Her friend Caroline cut her off. "But I've got some plants that could use watering once a week," she said. "That's not something the staff is supposed to do, but I usually forget and a few of them are dying. I don't know if I can pay you cash, but I could figure out some other way to make it worth your while."

"I wouldn't even need money!" Herb said quickly. "I like watering plants and I'd be happy to do it for you."

Great Aunt Lucinda laughed. "Maybe we could get you a name badge—one like Bernie's—so you look official and you can show your family that you have a job."

"I love Bernie's name tag!" Herb shrieked. Bernie's name tag was a big, solid navy rectangle with his name stamped on in giant white capital letters. Bernie had decorated the blank spaces on his tag with special heart stickers that fit his caring and loving personality. "I *really* want a name tag."

"It's not fair to have you do work without some kind of reward," Diane pointed out.

"A name tag is all I need," Herb said.

Diane tilted her head and said, "Well, I sure would love to have you come by and help me wash up a few mugs and dust under my pictures a few times a week."

"I can do that!" Herb said. He glanced at Joye to see if she had some odd jobs she also might want Herb to do. But Joye just scowled at him and pulled her eyebrows together. She didn't seem to like Herb very much, ever since he'd gotten a Bingo one afternoon when she was just one space away from winning herself. Herb looked quickly away; Joye was almost as scary as the shadows in their new mansion.

Aunt Lucinda said, "I bet I can work out an agreement with Bernie so your lobby watering and animal care are a little more official and regular . . ." She squeezed her lips into a thin line and said, "Maybe we can come up with a deal where you do some odd jobs around here in exchange for lunch."

Herb's eyes got wide. "You guys get the best lunch!

I definitely want to come when it's macaroni and cheese day. And when Chef Jo makes that yellow cake with chocolate frosting." Aunt Lucinda and her friends laughed again. Herb had another idea. "You know that little pool at the end of the hall?"

"The therapy pool?" Joye grumbled. "I can't stand that thing. Makes my skin itch, so I only go in when they make me."

"Do you think I could maybe swim in there sometimes?" Herb begged. "It's shallow, so they wouldn't have to worry about me drowning or anything. But I'm also a really good swimmer so they wouldn't have to worry about that anyway." Herb twisted his hands together, begging. "I love pools."

"I suppose if your dad would sign some sort of waiver," Great Aunt Lucinda said, obviously thinking it through. "I can look into it, anyway. Do you happen to have a résumé?"

"A *what*?" Herb asked.

"A résumé is something people use when they're trying to get a job. It's a piece of paper that lists your personal information, like your name and address and phone number, along with previous work experience and education. It makes you seem more professional when you're applying for a job."

Herb shrugged. "I don't have one, but I can make one right now if you think it would help me get the job." With help from the four ladies, Herb used his neatest handwriting and wrote out his very first résumé.

HERBERT PEACH
East 2nd Street
Duluth, Minnesota

WORK EXPERIENCE
- Mouse Caretaker
- Inventor of Herb's Cinnaballs™
- Peach Pie Truck Mascot
- 2nd Grade Classroom Hamster Feeder
- Dishwasher Unloader (only sometimes)
- Dog Trainer-in-Training

EDUCATION
- 3rd Grade Student at Lakeside Elementary School

The tip of Herb's tongue stuck out of the left corner of his mouth while he worked on his résumé. Once he'd written down all the jobs he'd had during the first eight and a half years of his life, he pushed the paper across the table for Great Aunt Lucinda to look over.

"This looks wonderful," she said. "I'll put in a good word with Bernie and the higher-ups, and we'll see if we can get you officially hired as the Birch Pond plant waterer and helper-outer. I'll act as your manager and see if we can work out some kind of compensation for your service."

Herb beamed. His first official *job*! So what if he didn't have a guest room of his very own to manage at the B&B . . . just wait until his family heard about *this*!

From the Sketchbook of Freddy Peach:
GREAT AUNT LUCINDA'S WIGS

The Dolly Parton

Grumpy old lady

The Purple Rain

Salt and pepper

Kind grandmother

Bowl of spaghetti

River of dreams

The Marge Simpson

The Rockstar

9

BREAKFAST PRACTICE

Freddy sat on the dirty floor of his new art shed, sketching more ideas for the upcoming art competition. He'd never been a traditional artist, and he had no plans to become one now. The trouble was Freddy hadn't yet decided which side of his artistic style to showcase for this particular contest. He already knew he was going to *build* a replica of his dream treehouse (the idea for which was inspired by one of his favorite books, *The 13-Story Treehouse*), rather than drawing, painting, or sculpting it. He loved making giant art installations that took up space, captured people's attention, and challenged him as a builder. But the big question was: Should he build his treehouse so it looked realistic? Futuristic and outer-spacey? Trash-like? Made out of food?

He had too many ideas, and too few easy decisions.

Between planning this art project design, the real-world Peach Pit renovation, and his family's plans for opening the B&B, he was also running very, very tight on time.

For years, Freddy had been sketching some of the rooms he'd want included in his dream treehouse— sketching was one of his favorite ways to shake ideas loose that were hiding or snoozing deep inside his brain. By now, he had a pretty good idea of what his treehouse invention would look and feel like in the *real* world. But this project would exist in the *art* world, so there were no limits to what he could create! Freddy's hand began to cramp up as he drew the pool-sized bathtub in his treehouse, so he decided to take a quick break and head inside the house for a snack.

He scanned the walk-in pantry, looking for something delicious to eat. There was almost nothing other than cans of tomatoes, packets of dried pasta, a couple giant containers of miscellaneous baking supplies that were still left over from their food truck summer, and a few boxes of macaroni and cheese—no granola bars, no candy, no cookies, no nuts, nothin'. So he turned to the fridge, where he found a carton of milk, some buttermilk, a plastic container of blueberries, and some butter. Nothing quick and easy to eat. Luckily, Freddy had learned to cook a few things while they were on their road trip that summer, and decided he might as well whip up a batch of blueberry buttermilk pancakes. It was one of his (only) specialties.

While he cooked, Freddy jotted down a few more ideas for foods they could serve for breakfast at the B&B. He, Lucy, and Herb had been working on a list of their favorite breakfast foods for the past week. Now, Freddy added blueberry scones, blueberry pancakes, and Dutch baby pancakes (which were these cool, egg-y pancake thingies that got cooked in an iron skillet and came out of the oven all puffy and amazing and buttery).

With construction and plumbing and electrical work in full swing at the Peach Pit, Freddy decided now would be the perfect time to really start thinking about the details for the *second* B in *bed-and-breakfast*. After their summer adventure running the Peach Pie Truck and camping and eating dinner at campgrounds on the road, the Peach family had plenty of experience cooking and preparing and serving food together. And luckily, they would be hiring an employee—a B&B *host*—who could help cook and serve and welcome guests. But Freddy wasn't willing to give up all control to a non-Peach, so he had every intention of guiding the plans for the logistics of *how* they would welcome guests, from check-in to checkout.

After doing a bit of research, Freddy realized that the key to a popular inn was *great* food and service. It was good news that they could make *food*, but they needed more than *just* food—they needed *cuisine* (which Freddy had recently learned was a word that kind of meant fancy food).

After scanning hundreds (possibly *thousands*) of internet reviews, Freddy had discovered that people could spend the night in an actual *castle*, but customer reviews were almost always brutal if the food or service was only *meh*. So a good breakfast service would be key to his family succeeding as the owners of Duluth's newest B&B.

Since they would only be serving *breakfast* at the B&B, and guests would be on their own for lunch and dinner (the Peach Pit was a bed-and-breakfast, not bed-and-lunch or bed-and-Brussels-sprout-casserole), the Peaches were working on finalizing a list of foods they might serve—an old family apple muffin recipe, and eggs, and those yummy sausage links his friend Ethan's mom always made after sleepovers. They'd decided they should also serve something sort of like peach pie, since that was a family classic. Herb wanted to serve Herb's Cinnaballs, which were sort of like sugar doughnuts—but made out of pie crust instead of dough. Lucy argued that they needed to offer some sort of fruit, for nutritional purposes (blech!), and Dad had offered to be in charge of figuring out what kind of tea and coffee they would need to have on hand. Now, *what* to serve wasn't really worrying Freddy, but *how* they would serve breakfast to guests was a different matter.

Though the person they hired to help out would clean the guest rooms and cook and serve breakfast a lot of the time, Freddy wanted to be ready to be as hands-on as possible whenever he was home and could help out. He had always dreamed of being a waiter—the kind who wore one of those snazzy tuxedos and spoke in a fancy accent with a special dish towel tossed over one arm, bowing to customers after he took their order.

But being a *good* waiter took practice, he knew, so he decided to enlist his two best friends to help. Which is how, a few days later, on Sunday morning, his friends Ethan and Henry ended up sitting in front of full place settings on opposite ends of the Peaches' enormous dining room table.

"Welcome, welcome!" Freddy said in his best French accent, bowing to his two friends. He'd put on his only button-down shirt, which he'd gotten as a gift from Great Aunt Lucinda the previous year for a special dinner party she'd hosted at the mansion. The sleeves were too short, and Freddy had only ironed the front, since that's all anyone would see anyway—but he looked fancy enough. "I hope you are both very well!"

Ethan and Henry both snickered. "Why are you speaking with a bad Australian accent?" Henry giggled.

"I'm not," Freddy argued. "It's French."

"*Oui oui*," Ethan snorted. "*Wee wee*, hee hee."

Freddy turned away from them and rolled his eyes. This was supposed to be his practice for the real deal of serving guests their breakfast at the B&B, so he couldn't exactly make rude faces at his "customers." "Welcome, *mon amis!*"

"I'm not Amy," Ethan blurted. "I'm Ethan."

"*Amis* is French for 'friends,'" Freddy grunted. "Come on, guys, take this seriously!"

Ethan and Henry both cracked up as Henry tucked one of Great Aunt Lucinda's laciest cloth napkins into the front of his T-shirt like a bib.

Freddy presented them both with menus just as Lucy, Herb, and Dad wandered into the dining room with bowls of cereal. "What's going on here?" Dad asked.

"I'm practicing for our B and B breakfast service. I asked Henry and Ethan to help pretend to be real customers, so I can get some experience serving people,"

Freddy explained, wondering if he'd ever even get *started* with the breakfast service, or if they'd spend the whole morning just chatting about things. He waved his arm toward the other three members of his family and offered, "Would the three of you like to join these other paying guests at the table? Perhaps the five of you can chat about how you'll all be spending your day exploring our fine city of Duluth, Minnesota?"

"What's wrong with your voice?" Herb asked, furrowing his brow. "Are you getting sick?"

"And why would we explore Duluth?" Lucy added. "We live here."

"Ugh!" Freddy snapped. "I'm speaking in a French accent. It makes our breakfast seem fancier. And you're not *actually* going to explore Duluth—you're supposed to be pretending you're guests at the B and B! That's what people do when they eat breakfast at a bed-and-breakfast—they talk to other guests about dumb stuff like being tourists!"

Lucy and Dad both laughed. "Gotcha," Dad said, settling in at one of the open seats at the table. Freddy took his family's empty cereal bowls, then set plates in front of the new arrivals. Next, he carefully put out forks, knives, and spoons, just like the pictures of fancy place settings he'd found on the internet.

Dad pounded the table and cried out, "Who do I need to talk to in order to get a cup of coffee around here?"

Freddy frowned at him. His dad wasn't usually so . . . well, so *rude.*

Dad chuckled and whispered, "You said we're pretending to be real customers, right? If so, I want to pretend to be a *terrible* customer. It's good practice." He winked at Freddy.

"Gotcha," Freddy said, winking back. "You say you're in need of a coffee, sir?"

"By now, it probably would have been faster for me to just get up and make it myself!" Dad hollered.

Herb, Lucy, Henry, and Ethan all cracked up. Lucy only stopped laughing long enough to say, "Excuse me, but I believe this knife needs polishing?" She held up one of Great Aunt Lucinda's old-fashioned silver knives and scowled at Freddy.

Freddy swiped the knife from his sister and replaced it with a shinier one. He hadn't even gotten their drinks, and Freddy was already fed up with serving people. Hopefully, real guests wouldn't act as awful as his own family and friends were! He hightailed it into the kitchen and got a pitcher of orange juice, along with a cup of coffee that his dad had actually brewed for himself earlier that morning.

When he set down the fresh-squeezed orange juice, Herb scowled at him. "I don't like pulp."

"You love pulp," Freddy argued.

"My *character* doesn't like pulp," Herb said. "What other drinks do you have?"

"Um." Freddy hadn't prepared any alternatives to orange juice. "We have Duluth's finest water, coffee, and ice water."

"You're offering us water or *ice* water?" Henry scoffed. "That's exactly the same thing. This feels like a scam! I need to speak with your manager." He and Ethan both laughed.

"Do you have comment cards?" Ethan said, snorting. Then he whispered, "Being a bad customer is the best."

Freddy huffed, trying to ignore the annoying comments spewing from the table. He hustled into the kitchen and grabbed the basket of apple muffins he'd baked that morning, along with a bowl of scrambled eggs and a platter of bacon. Sadly, the eggs and bacon were probably lukewarm (at best) by now, but it's all he had to offer. He hustled back into the dining room and set the food in the center of the table with a flourish.

His best friends both dove for the muffin basket, shoving them whole into their mouths and grabbing a second before his family had even taken one each. "These are yummy," Henry said. Freddy grinned. It was the first nice thing anyone had said all morning.

Dad nodded as he delicately ripped chunks off the muffin. "They really are delicious," he agreed. "You might have just gotten yourself a job as the breakfast baker in our B and B, Fred."

Herb huffed out an angry breath; Freddy knew his little brother got frustrated when Freddy and Lucy were assigned projects that he wasn't asked to do. Like the guest room thing—Herb was super mad he had to share the responsibility for cleaning, repairing, and decorating one of the rooms with their dad. But the thing Freddy had realized over the past week was, Herb ought to be relieved! Freddy had already spent hours cleaning "The Freddy Suite" (as he'd been calling it), and had quickly discovered just how much more time it would take to:

1. Figure out the theme of his room (he'd come up with ideas, but none of them seemed quite right and his brain was swirling with decisions he needed to make about this *and* his art competition piece!)
2. Clean the room *more* and make sure all the bathroom parts were working (and afterward, talk to the plumber and carpenter and stuff about all the things that *weren't* working)
3. Order all the right decorations and sheets and stuff

Freddy was *not* an interior decorator, and he kind of wished he hadn't asked to be in charge of one of the guest rooms at all. It was a pain, and he'd made almost no progress; Lucy's guest room was coming along nicely, but the The Freddy Suite was a torn-apart disaster. He'd rather handle customer service stuff; that's what he was truly good at. Also, between his art project, his guest room details, and helping to fix stuff around the mansion, he was feeling kind of . . . overwhelmed. He'd never admit it to the rest of his family, but Freddy was starting to wonder if he'd bitten off more projects than he could handle, and now it was hard to chew everything.

Both Herb and Lucy polished off their muffins and

reached for the eggs and bacon. Freddy was relieved the muffins were a hit. Wait until they tried his Dutch baby pancakes!

Just as Freddy was starting to feel pretty confident that maybe he *could* get the hang of this waiter business, Herb grouchily blurted out, "Is there a strange smell in here? My nose is acting up. Do you happen to have . . . dogs? I'm highly allergic."

COUSIN MILLIE'S
FAMOUS APPLE MUFFINS

- ○ 2 eggs
- ○ 1/2 C vegetable oil
- ○ 1 C milk
- ○ 1 t vanilla
- ○ 1/2 C brown sugar
- ○ 1/2 C applesauce (optional)
- ○ 1 T baking powder
- ○ 1/2 t salt
- ○ 1 t nutmeg
- ○ 1 t cinnamon
- ○ 1 t allspice (optional)
- ○ 1 large apple (diced)

1. Preheat oven to 400° F.
2. Mix all the wet stuff—except the apple chunks—together in a bowl. In a separate bowl, mix all the dry ingredients together. Fold the dry ingredients into the mixed wet ingredients and stir. Do not overmix! Gently stir in the apple chunks. Put batter into a muffin tin—either greased or with muffin liners. Fill muffin tins about 2/3 full.

3. Bake for 10–15 minutes, or until a toothpick stuck into the center of a muffin comes out clean.

   OPTIONAL: Top with a crumb topping mixture before you put muffins in the oven:
   - **1/2 C flour**
   - **1/4 C butter chopped up into tiny bits**
   - **1/4 C brown sugar**

10

A STROLL DOWN MEMORY LANE

Nearly another full week passed before Lucy finally got to revisit her secret, hidden attic space.

She'd spent every day after school that week meeting with her dad and either the plumber, the electrician, or the "Handy Gals" to talk through construction projects. Lucy liked being a part of these meetings, since it made her feel important. She also found that if she was in the room, meetings tended to move more quickly—her dad often got bogged down in little details and liked to know a little *too* much about how things worked.

But mostly, she loved spending time with the two college women who were doing most of the carpentry work in the Peach Pit. They called themselves the Handy Gals, and both were in the forestry program at the university. One of the Handy Gals—Lila—was the daughter of one of Dad's coworkers, and the other—Kassy—was her best friend. Lucy hoped someday *she'd* have a job where she could work alongside her best friend all day. Whenever the Handy Gals were in the house, Lucy learned a ton of interesting information about carpentry *and* forestry. Unlike all the random facts Freddy was always spouting out, these women's fun facts seemed like they might actually come in useful at some point in Lucy's future.

Unfortunately, being as involved as she was in these meetings, Lucy had learned that nearly all of the money Dad had planned to use for the renovation (the $75,000, give or take, that they had left over in the fun-money pot after selling the Peach Pie Truck) had already been spent on the work they'd planned first. The house was crumbling in many places, and there were far more problems hidden inside the walls and pipes than any of them had expected. Dad had dipped into his emergency-money fund for a couple plumbing surprises, but he'd already said if any *more* surprises came up, they would need to call the whole project off.

Every time they talked to the never-ending stream of construction people who seemed to be living in the house alongside them, her dad tugged a little more hair out of his already balding head. Lucy knew her dad was really stressed about money, which made her worry. What if they had to stop work and the B&B could never open? What if they had to move out and let someone else move in? What if they had to go back to their old life, the one they'd been living in before the first Great Peach Experiment? Even if their lives weren't exactly *normal*, it had felt good to feel like a family again these past few months.

Lucy had been making good progress on her guest room, which she was officially calling "The Winter Suite." The bathroom attached to The Winter Suite was finally working the way it was supposed to (no more brown water or toilet that needed to be jiggled to flush), since the plumber and Handy Gals had focused on finishing up her guest room first. Once all the messy work was done, Lucy had cleaned the room, washed the windows, and had already ordered beautiful icy blue bedding and throw pillows that were covered in sparkly snowflakes. She was planning to steal some decorations and vases and hopefully some art from the boxes up in the attic.

Earlier that week, Lucy and Herb had emailed one of their mom's old coworkers to ask for help installing some of Mom's solar window clings in the guest rooms at the B&B. Those would be coming in a few weeks, so

Lucy felt like she was on task and on target; but hers was the *only* guest room anywhere close to ready. Much as she wanted to step in and take over Freddy's guest room project, instead she started making a list of all the other things they'd need to have in each room before anyone came to stay:

STUFF GUESTS LIKE:

Shampoo
Conditioner
Lotion
Soap
Fluffy towels
Slippers
Comfy pillows
Robes

Lucy hadn't stayed in a lot of hotels, but she had stayed in a few during some of Dad's science conventions. Enough to know they were supposed to be comfortable and feel like a second home, but also be a little nicer (with the added bonus of having someone clean your room and make your bed for you).

Late Sunday afternoon, while Herb was off visiting

Great Aunt Lucinda (which he seemed to be doing a lot more frequently over the past week), Freddy was busy working in his art shed, and Dad had snuck off to the lab to wrap up some things he hadn't finished at work that week, Lucy finally got a chance to crawl up into the attic again. Before doing anything else, she dragged the big dollhouse over to the trapdoor into her closet and carefully lowered it down onto the ledge below. She wanted to surprise Herb with something special, and it was silly to waste a beautiful dollhouse by keeping it hidden up here where no one could enjoy it. She hadn't yet come up with an explanation for *where* she'd found the dollhouse, since she wanted to keep the attic a secret for herself, but she'd figure that out later.

After she'd lowered the giant dollhouse down into her closet, Lucy shuffled back across the attic to dig around in more boxes. As she pushed aside yet another bin of Christmas decorations, Lucy noticed another, smaller box of photos she hadn't seen the last time she'd been up in the attic. The picture at the top of the stack was of her parents on their wedding day. Both of her parents were beaming, and Dad had all his hair. Lucy dug deeper into the box, pulling out more wedding pictures as well as some pictures of her parents that looked like they'd been taken even before they were married.

Down at the bottom of the box, Lucy found an album filled with childhood pictures of her mom. She wondered if Dad had been hiding these here, at Great Aunt Lucinda's house, to keep him from having to think about her more than he already did.

Lucy felt tears spring to her eyes as she pawed through pictures of her mom at her high school graduation; holding up a giant trophy with a group of other girls; beaming as she held a piece of paper with a sonogram picture of a baby. (Was that Lucy when she was in her mom's tummy? She had a feeling it probably was.) Eventually, maybe, she'd share these pictures with her brothers—but for now, she was going to keep them for herself. She knew it was probably selfish, but she didn't want to tell anyone else about them yet. She desperately wanted a little more alone time with her mom.

Digging deeper into the boxes, Lucy unearthed really old pictures of Great Aunt Lucinda from *her* childhood. Lucy was surprised to realize how much she resembled her great aunt—they had the same smile and speckled greenish-brown eyes from Dad's side of the family, but Great Aunt Lucinda had straight blond hair like Dad's, while Lucy's was thick and brown like her Mom's and brothers'. It was so interesting to dig into so much Peach family history. Think of all the fun stories there were trapped inside these musty old boxes!

It was more than an hour later when Lucy heard Herb's little voice cry out to her through the intercom from downstairs in the kitchen. "Luuuuuuucy!" Herb liked to know where everyone was the moment he walked in the back door.

Shoot! Lucy had to get out of the attic before he made it up to the fourth floor, or he'd discover her hiding spot. By the time Herb and the dogs came tromping up the final set of stairs, Lucy had pulled the giant dollhouse into the center of her bedroom and draped a spare sheet over the top of it. Before Herb could ask her any questions about why she hadn't answered his intercom call, Lucy yelled out, "Surprise! I have a present for you."

Herb stared at the sheet-covered, three-foot-tall lump. "What is it?"

"Uncover it and find out."

He pulled the sheet off with a flourish. "It's a mini version of the Peach Pit!" Herb whooped as he circled around the dollhouse for a view of all sides. "It's so pretty. Where'd you find it?"

"It was just sitting in one of the old servant staircases," Lucy said, a little concerned by how easily the lie had slipped off her tongue. But saying the dollhouse had been inside one of the servant staircases was as good an explanation as any; she was the only member of the family who ever used the twisty staircases tucked within the walls, so it *could* be true. "I brought it out for you. I thought you might like to decorate it and maybe keep some of your treasures inside?"

Herb wrapped his spindly little arms around her in a hug. "I love it, Lulu. Thank you."

Lucy squeezed him back, wondering: Was telling her brother one little lie really *so* bad if it was delivered with a gift?

11

FIRST DAY ON THE JOB

Herb absolutely *loved* the dollhouse Lucy had found for him. Somehow, getting a chance to peek inside a miniature version of their new house made the giant, life-sized mansion feel a little less scary. He adored the colorful framed fruit art glued to the walls in each of the dollhouse's rooms, and he loved that he could see inside every corner of the house all at once. Best of all, Herb could arrange it so nothing and no one was ever left alone inside any rooms in the giant house. He'd already filled the rooms with little rock monsters and some of his smallest stuffed animals and figurines. It had taken some time for him to find them buried deep in his packed boxes, but as soon as he dug them out, he'd also filled the rooms with some of the LEGO figurines he and his mom had used when they used to play the game Restaurant with an old plastic food truck.

Herb had found the perfect spot to set up his new dollhouse, right on the long wooden bench on the first-floor stair landing. It sat in the exact spot where Lucy had told him his mom used to love to sit and read. There was a nice view of the overgrown flowers in the side yard, and the colored stained glass in the windows created fun triangles and squares of different colors on the floor and walls on the landing. The Peaches had brought Mom's favorite throw pillow with them from their other house, the one that was embroidered with one of her favorite phrases: WHEN LIFE GIVES YOU LEMONS, MAKE ICED TEA. Having it here in the house with them, perched on the wooden reading seat in the giant window of Great Aunt Lucinda's mansion, made it seem like a little piece of Mom had moved with them.

Since Herb was little when Mom died, he didn't have as many memories stored up as his brother and sister did. So he loved having a few *things* around that helped him keep her memory alive. This was part of the reason Herb loved *stuff* and his collections in general—holding on to special things helped him remember good times.

In the few days after Lucy gave him the dollhouse, Herb used a bunch of construction junk he found around the house to personalize his mini-mansion with leftover fabric, torn-out wallpaper, and furniture made of wood scraps and building materials and other stuff he found. Once Herb had dressed it up with some of his own decorations, the dollhouse felt full and happy and uniquely *Herb*. The best part was *this* was a renovation project he was allowed to do all on his own, without Dad or Lucy or Freddy partnering with him, and that made it even more special. He finally had some rooms of his own to manage and organize.

Each night before bed, Herb would set up all the people and furniture inside the house and tuck everything in for the night. Then he'd let the dogs out for their last-chance pee and race upstairs to the fourth floor to snuggle into his tiny bedroom tucked in right beside Lucy's. Life in the mansion was starting to grow on him, and Herb now felt the same pull to stay in this special new home as his siblings did.

The next weekend, Herb had his first official shift at Birch Pond. When he showed up for work, Great Aunt Lucinda and her friends were waiting to welcome him in the front room. Herb greeted them all with a curt handshake and said, "Herb Peach, reporting for duty."

All the ladies—except Joye—laughed and patted him on the back and squeezed his cheeks and told him he was a cutie. Herb bristled, but smiled in a professional way. "Where would you like me to start?"

"Well," Great Aunt Lucinda said, glancing over at Bernie, who was standing tall behind the welcome desk. "Before anything, we need to make this official."

For a second, Herb wondered if he had papers to sign, or had to put his hand on a Bible and take some kind of oath like people did in court. But before he could wonder long, Bernie stepped out from behind the desk and held up a shiny blue name tag with HERB printed on it in bright white letters. "For you, my man," Bernie said, pinning it to Herb's shirt.

Herb grinned. His very own official name tag. He was a working man!

Over the next two hours, Herb worked hard at his new job. He fed the fish and turtles. He watered the plants in the lobby and in all the common areas in the Birch Pond retirement complex. He picked up litter he found in the hallways. But the best part of his job, by far, was stopping in different people's apartments to help them with odd jobs. Some residents wanted him to water their plants and a few asked him to dust (this was *super* fun, because Bernie had provided him with a very fancy and fluffy feather duster!). Then there were a number of residents who had asked Herb to stop by not because they had any specific *task* for him, but because they just wanted to talk or share a joke or offer him a snack.

During his shift, Herb was given wrapped candies, a maple doughnut, and several cups of milk and juice—but he was offered much *much* more than that. Even sweeter, Herb was also given small tips and gifts by many of the residents to thank him for his service. He got a little bell from Caroline, some fizzy bath salts from Diane, a snuggly sleep mask from a man named Jim, a full box of stickers from a lady named Helen, and a collection of colorful buttons from a guy called Lou. One woman, Trudie, told him he could choose—and keep!—one stuffed Beanie Baby toy from her massive collection *every single time* he stopped by. Herb's treasure bins would be stuffed full to bursting after just a few shifts at Birch Pond!

After he'd finished up all his tasks for the day, he joined Great Aunt Lucinda and her friends for lunch. They were having meatloaf and mashed potatoes, which were not Herb's favorite but somehow tasted wonderful after all the sweets he'd eaten that morning.

"How's school going so far this year?" Aunt Lucinda asked him over dessert (a slice of apple pie, which Herb politely refused). Herb was having a hard time taking his great aunt seriously, since today she was wearing a straight, long, bright purple wig that made her skin glow very white. Most of the time, she wore wigs that more closely resembled actual old lady hair. This purple one was a strange new addition to his great aunt's crazy-days wig collection.

"It's pretty good," Herb said. He told her about his teacher's book club, and some of the other fun things Mr. Andrus had planned for the class that year. "But there is one thing I'm a little sad about."

Caroline scooted closer to him, concern splashed across her face. "You don't seem like the kind of guy who gets *sad* very often."

"I'm not," Herb agreed. "But the thing is—" He broke off, hating having to talk about this out loud. "My teacher plans a special tea party every year."

"That sounds like it would be right up your alley," Diane said, her eyebrows pulled together.

Herb nodded. "It is! But the thing is, it's a Mother-Son Tea. And I . . . well, I don't have a mother. Not anymore."

All four women—even grouchy Joye—clucked and sighed. "That can't be a hard-and-fast rule," Great Aunt Lucinda muttered. "Have you asked your teacher if you can bring someone else? There must be some sort of work-around to make this fair to everyone."

"No, I haven't asked about that," Herb admitted. "I will." But Herb already knew he *wouldn't*. Because he wasn't the kind of person who broke rules, and he didn't like to cause problems. He already had to leave school early two days a week to get to his special advanced math course at the university, and his classmates were always giving him funny looks when he was called down to the office when his dad got there to pick him up. That was enough special attention for him, and he certainly wasn't going to make himself stick out even *more* by trying to break the rules at his teacher's special tea party.

But that didn't mean it hurt any less.

"I have good news, though!" he said, hoping to change the subject. The ladies all stared at him expectantly. "Dasher and I took a walk around the block—on a *leash*—yesterday! He's making really good progress, and he might get to come by for a visit soon. Vix is pretty good at sitting when I tell her to, but the other dogs still have a ways to go. Last night I caught Donner carrying around a whole loaf of bread. He only ate a couple pieces, but he took little bites out of the rest of the loaf and scattered slices all around the house to eat later."

Great Aunt Lucinda snickered. "I miss those little treasures."

"Behavior like that sounds like a nightmare to me," Joye grumbled.

Herb frowned. "They're sweet," he argued. "I'm going to bring a couple of them down here soon to visit and you can see how great they are."

Joye lifted an eyebrow. "Mm-hmm," she grunted. "I'll believe *that* when I see it."

Herb propped his elbows on the table and dropped his chin into his hands. No matter what he said, Joye just did not seem to like him. And Herb didn't like when people didn't like him.

"Elbows off the table during meals," Joye said, glaring at him.

Herb stuffed his hands into his lap and smiled sheepishly back at her. He was determined to win Joye over . . . eventually. By Thanksgiving, he vowed. By the time they opened the B&B, he would make sure the dogs were well-enough behaved that they would be ready for a visit to Birch Pond *and* ready to share the mansion with paying guests. They would charm everyone, Herb decided—even mean old Joye.

WHAT CAN YOU GROW
OUT OF A PEACH PIT?

FREDDY'S TREEHOUSE
"Food Room"

12

FREDDY'S PRANK

These were some of the things Freddy had recently discovered to be true:

1. Turtles could breathe out of their butts.
2. A Phillips-head screwdriver was shaped like this:

and a flat-head screwdriver was shaped like this:

(These are the kinds of things you learn when you live in a construction zone.)

3. Great Aunt Lucinda's old mansion was a total Peach Pit, but Freddy hadn't yet given up hope that they could grow it into something lovely again. (The big question at the moment was: Would they really *ever* be ready for strangers who would have to *pay* to stay there?!)

4. Freddy had always been allergic to cats, but he'd just learned that *some cats are actually allergic to humans*!

5. His new house had seven bedrooms, seven bathrooms, a kitchen, a "butler's pantry," a formal dining room, an eat-in breakfast nook, a living room, a study/piano room (with no piano), a seemingly endless number of staircases and mysterious doors, and far, *far* too many places where mice could be hiding.

6. There were mice living somewhere inside the mansion. He could just *feel* it. (Because of this, Freddy was always very careful to make a lot of noise—singing, burping, or stomping— as he traveled up and down the mansion's central staircase or moved from room to room. The louder he was, he reasoned, the more likely it was he could scare away any small,

pointy-teeth creatures who might be hanging out, munching on crumbs, waiting to leap out and attack him.

7. He had a *lot* of work to do if his art project was going to be ready for the citywide competition and show. All he had at the moment were a bunch of ideas and sketches, and that wasn't gonna cut it. (Trouble was, Dad kept reminding him that his schoolwork had to come first—before he was allowed to work on his art, or the Peach Pit, or baking things. After he got a 42 percent on his first math test of the year, he was now required to get Dad or Lucy to sign off on his homework before he was allowed to spend any time out in his art shed each day. Freddy found this infuriating.)

8. Competitive art used to be a category in the Olympics.

9. Freddy Peach baked the best blueberry scones on earth. So good, in fact, that they could easily win a gold medal in the Olympics if *that* ever became a category. (Would *competitive baking* be a Summer Olympics category, or Winter? Winter, Freddy decided. Definitely the Winter Olympics.)

10. The blob of toothpaste that gets plopped on top of your toothbrush has an actual, official name! It's called a "nurdle" (and somehow, knowing this made Freddy actually enjoy brushing his teeth for the first time in his life). In other random-fact news, he'd also recently discovered the dot over a lowercase *i* and *j* is called a "tittle." This, too, was endlessly fascinating. He couldn't help but wonder: Whose job was it to name these kinds of random things? Was that a job *Freddy* could get someday?!

11. Freddy had just devised the very best prank *ever* to play on his little brother.

Herb was completely obsessed with the dollhouse that Lucy had found somewhere deep in the mansion's creepy, twisting servant staircases. Over the past few weeks, while the rest of the family worked with the Handy Gals and electricians and a never-ending stream of plumbers to repair the skin, bone, and guts of the mansion (as well as the more boring tasks of painting, organizing, and cleaning guest rooms and common areas), Herb had spent hours decorating his *mini* Peach Pit and futzing around with his LEGO figurines to set the house up *just so*. Whenever Freddy walked by during the day, he liked to move something around inside—just to see if Herb would notice.

Herb always noticed. Just like with his boxes and bins of collections, Herb was particular about what went where. He was *so* particular about his dollhouse arrangement, in fact, that he'd started using Dad's phone to take pictures of each room in the mini Peach Pit before he went to bed at night to have it on record. Herb's obsession with order was what gave Freddy the perfect idea for a prank.

From the time he was a baby, Herb had been afraid of Great Aunt Lucinda's mansion. He was convinced it was haunted, and all the funny noises the house made didn't help at all. Freddy had discovered it was easy to hide just around a corner and pop out to surprise his little brother, eliciting a scream so loud that it set all the dogs to barking at once.

With Halloween on the horizon, creepy decorations had been popping up in yards all over their new neighborhood. So ghosts and goblins were top-of-mind for Herb, and Freddy had a little something special planned to totally spook his brother in the most hilarious way possible.

One Friday night at dinner, right in the middle

of October, Freddy set the stage for his prank. "Have any of you guys heard that weird moaning in the wall behind the first-floor stair landing?" he asked his dad, Lucy, and Herb through a mouthful of mashed potatoes (the kind from a box).

Herb's mouth dropped open, revealing a mass of white mush inside. His eyes grew wide. "Moaning?" he whispered.

"Maybe it's more *groaning*," Freddy said with a shrug. "I found the dogs all sitting in front of the wall right by Herb's dollhouse, barking at something yesterday. Then Dasher started sniffing and scratching at the wall. It was weird." He tried to hide a grin. "But I'm sure it's nothing."

"Pipes," Dad said, grabbing a roll off the plate in the middle of the table. "Our pipes make an awful racket."

Lucy glanced at Herb and said in a lighthearted voice, "I'm sure it's just the pipes."

Dad heaved a sigh. "We really should get the plumber to take a look at that and see if she can get back there and tighten some stuff up."

For a moment, Freddy felt a little guilty for dropping yet another to-do in his dad's lap. But he knew they couldn't actually afford any *shoulds* at the moment— they could only afford the *must-do* projects—so he'd clear things up before Dad ever actually put a plumber on the case.

"Do you guys want to know how we're doing on our to-do list?" Lucy suddenly blurted out, obviously trying to change the subject before Herb got even more freaked out.

Freddy glanced at his little brother, who was now pushing mounds of potato mush around his plate. Freddy could tell the stage had been perfectly set to put his plan into action. Coughing to hide a giggle, Freddy said, "We're making progress. The living room is done, right?"

For the next twenty minutes, they talked about all the projects around the mansion that were finished.

They had completed the living room, cleaned up the dining room and china cabinets, and fixed all the loose floorboards and doorknobs.

The outdoor window trim had been repaired and painted—but not well. Dad had decided they would handle that project all on their own and, with the exception of Freddy, none of them knew their way around a paintbrush. Also, they were still trying to wash all the little painted paw prints off the front walkway, which had been there since several of the pups had also tried to "help" with the project.

One weekend they'd spent what felt like a thousand

hours deep-cleaning the kitchen and pantry, which was one of the worst weekends of Freddy's entire life.

Lucy's Winter Suite was coming along nicely, so they had at least one room mostly ready for guests.

And they'd interviewed a bunch of college kids who were interested in a part-time job as their B&B "host." The job would involve helping out with guest services when the Peaches were at work or school or didn't have the time to manage the day-to-day operation of the B&B themselves. They had all easily agreed on hiring a smiley guy named Theo who had actually lived and worked in an old historic inn in Connecticut as a kid and he totally loved dogs! It didn't *hurt* his chances that Theo was also a Cardboard Camp counselor, which made him a true hero in Freddy's book.

"It's a good thing we're in pretty good shape," Dad said with a slight smile. "Because I have exciting news!"

Freddy had learned that *exciting news* in Dad-speak could mean any number of things: that he'd found a missing sock in the bottom of the laundry, or that his favorite flavor of iced tea was back in stock at the university quick mart, or that they were going to be taking a trip to Iceland. You never knew which level of *exciting* Dad was talking about at any given time.

"We have our first guest coming to stay next weekend!" Dad said, clapping.

Lucy coughed out a mouthful of milk. "A real, paying guest?"

"Sort of," Dad said. "She's not paying, but I got an email from Lois Sibberson earlier this week, and she's on her way to sell baked goods at some sort of fall festival up in Ely. She's going to be driving through town with the truck and asked if we'd be willing to have her swing by for a visit."

"Lois Sibberson, the lady who bought the Peach Pie Truck off us at the Ohio Food Truck Festival this summer?" Freddy asked. *"That* Lois Sibberson?"

"That's the one," Dad confirmed. "I thought it would be fun to invite her to stay and check out our next Great Peach Experiment."

"She can stay in The Winter Suite!" Lucy quickly offered. "I can have it ready by next weekend for sure."

"Think we can have our breakfast plan figured out by then?" Dad asked, looking specifically toward Freddy.

Freddy flushed with pride. "Definitely. I'll make blueberry scones. I bet Lois will ask me for my recipe, so she can sell some just like it out of her food truck."

As they cleaned up dinner and talked about the plans for Lois and the Peach Pie Truck's visit, Herb was much more quiet than usual. For a few moments, Freddy felt bad for planting more scary thoughts in his head. But Herb was always begging to be treated like a big kid (and Freddy had even overheard him telling their sister he was much more mature and adult-like than *Freddy*, which really peeved him). Only little kids were afraid of ghosts and spooky noises, so Freddy was really doing Herb a *favor* by helping him conquer his fear that the mansion was haunted. It would just take a little time to do that, that's all.

That night before bed, Freddy offered to read with Herb to help him get to sleep. This was usually Lucy's task, but she was happy to hand over the reins for a night, so she could do extra homework (or whatever it was she usually did on a Friday night). Before Freddy had even gotten to the end of the chapter in *The Vanderbeekers of 141st Street*, Herb had nodded off. Freddy poked his brother's foot, then his cheek, to be absolutely sure he was sound asleep.

As soon as he knew his brother was down for the count, Freddy quietly tiptoed down the stairs to the second-floor landing. Giggling quietly to himself, he carefully lifted several LEGO figurines from their places in the house, swapped their heads for LEGO monster heads Freddy had found in his own LEGO bin, and dropped the new creepy LEGO people right back into the same spots. Then he took the contents of the dollhouse's living room and swapped them with the contents of the kitchen, being careful to set up each room exactly the way it had been in Herb's original design—just in a totally different room within the mini-mansion.

As soon as he'd finished, he brushed his sweaty palms on his pants. Mission accomplished. Knowing Herb and his silly fear that the mansion was haunted, Freddy had absolutely no doubt his brother would assume the moaning ghost in the wall was now haunting his dollhouse. A little mean? Maybe. But funny? Most definitely.

TO-DO LIST: The Peach Pit

1. ~~Hire a plumber~~
   To do: lots of broken faucets, pee-stain leak under second-floor bedroom tub, ~~kitchen sink~~, brown water in showers, random moaning in walls???
2. Fix ~~broken door handles and~~ stair rail banisters
3. ~~Paint trim around the windows outside~~
4. ~~Fix/repair those sections of lizard-skin siding~~
5. ~~Peel off living room wallpaper and paint~~
6. Paint and repair guest room walls
7. ~~Clean and paint dining room~~
8. Replace cracked windows   <- TOO Expensive!
9. Clean guest bathrooms (after plumber is gone)
   — will he EVER be done??
10. ~~Mop floors & wash windows~~ ←

Convince Herb these things are fun

HOW TO OPEN A B&B

1. Plan & buy stuff to put in guest rooms
   Shampoo, Conditioner, Robes??, Bedding,
   Pillows, Slippers?, New art?
2. Organize and rearrange and clean guest room
   furniture
3. Clean guest bathrooms (after plumber is gone)
4. Figure out how to take reservations, check
   guests in when they show up, collect money,
   buy breakfast supplies, ~~do permit and business research,~~ and other important details like
   that
   ** ~~Hire our B&B host to help figure all this stuff out!!~~ <- I'm on it
5. Name the B&B   <- What's wrong wit
6. Mop floors & wash windows (Again!)   The Peach Pi
7. Figure out what we're going to offer guests
   for breakfast (since we have to offer the
   second <u>B</u> part of the B&B, not just a bed)
   IDEAS ARE COOKING!
8. ~~Practice serving breakfast~~
9. ~~Get tuxedoes so we can pretend to be butlers and act like we're working at a castle~~ ← NO!

10. Get ~~all the~~ ^more^ extra stuff to make the guest rooms feel homey: Shampoo, Conditioner, Lotion, Soap, ~~Fluffy towels~~, Slippers, ~~Comfy Pillows~~, Robes, Duluth books, <u>Midwest Mansions</u> book that includes the Peach Pit (?!)
11. Make a B&B website

13

THE FIRST GUEST

Lucy heard the familiar clanking sound of their family's old food truck out in the driveway. They'd been expecting Lois Sibberson, a retired teacher from Delaware, Ohio, to arrive in Duluth sometime that Friday. Ever since she'd gotten home from school for the day, Lucy had been waiting impatiently in the kitchen for their first official B&B guest to arrive. Now, she peeked out the window, watching as Lois eased the giant beast of a vehicle into their driveway and parked it beside the giant construction dumpster next to the garage— easily taking up nearly half of the massive driveway. Lucy announced Lois's arrival to her brothers and dad through the intercom, then ran outside to greet her.

"Welcome, Ms. Sibberson!" Lucy called out, waving at Lois through the driver's side window.

Lois hopped out of the truck. "Hi, hon. How's it feel to see this old friend again?" she asked, patting the side of the giant food truck affectionately.

"It looks almost exactly the same," Lucy noted. "Just fancier." The truck was still the same bright peachy-orange color it had been when Lucy's family had owned it, but Lois had gotten a fancy food truck wrap to cover up the truck's previous name. Where the side of the truck had once been emblazoned with THE PEACH PIE TRUCK in swirly, hand-painted letters, it now had a gorgeous illustration of muffins and cookies in a basket, along with the words BAKED WITH LOVE BY GRANDMA LOIS.

"Can I look inside?" Lucy asked.

"Be my guest," Lois told her. "I haven't changed a thing on the inside."

Lucy went around back and climbed up into the familiar space. While she ran her hands across the countertops, peeked inside the giant ovens, fondly thinking back on some of the incredible adventures they'd had that summer, Lois chattered away. She told Lucy about her drive up from Ohio and her plans for the fall festival in Ely she was heading to early the next morning. She wandered around the outside of the mansion and peeked into the sprawling nature preserve backyard.

"This is quite a house," Lois said, whistling as she took it all in. "What are you calling the place?"

"Freddy calls it the Peach Pit," Lucy said. "Since it's kind of falling apart."

Lois snorted just as the other three members of the Peach family came parading out of the mansion's back door. Lois waved at the guys, muttering to Lucy under her breath, "'The Peach Pit' doesn't exactly say *'cozy B and B'* to me. You might want to reconsider that."

Freddy had obviously overheard her, since he called out, "It's a working title," and held out a hand for Lois to shake. "It's great to see you again, Lois. Welcome to our home; *your* home away from home!"

"Thank you, Freddy," Lois said, chuckling. "It's good to see all your smiling faces again, too."

"Can I collect your bags?" Herb offered with a stiff bow. Lucy could tell that Freddy had been coaching their little brother on the ins and outs of being a good host. But obviously, Freddy had gone a bit overboard, and both brothers were now acting like fuddy-duddy butlers in some sort of eighteenth-century castle. "Would you like an icy cold glass of cucumber water?"

"Ooh la la," Lois said. "Cucumber water, eh? Very fancy."

"Can I take your coat?" Freddy said, using the same

weird accent as he had on the day they'd done their practice breakfast service with Ethan and Henry. "Would you like me to show you to the sitting room?" He took a step closer to Lois and offered her his arm.

"You've got a sitting room?" Lois hooted. She patted her fleece and said, "And this isn't a coat, it's a shirt."

"How do you take your tea?" Herb asked, crowding in even closer. Now *he* was using an accent that made him sound like a vampire.

Lois took a step back. "I think I'm good."

Lucy cringed. This whole butler routine was starting to feel very awkward. Her brothers were going to need to cool it a little bit, or they'd scare off all their guests by smothering them with *too* much hospitality.

"Come on in, Lois," their dad said. "We'll show you to your room and let you get settled. As I mentioned in my email, you're our first official guest here at the B and B. We're still working out some kinks and details of how things will actually run around here."

"We just hired someone who's going to help us out, but he hasn't started yet," Lucy explained. "So you're stuck with just us."

"Fine by me. Seems like you're off to a good start," Lois said kindly, trailing behind them into the house. "But as I said before, you might want to work on your

B and B name—'The Peach Pit' doesn't exactly have a charming ring to it."

Just as Lois stepped inside the back door, all four dogs rushed at her in one furry pack. They jumped and yipped and crowded around her legs, nearly knocking her into the shiny new stainless-steel kitchen counter.

"Dasher! Donner! Vix! Rudy!" Herb barked back at them in a stern voice. The four dogs paused in their yipping and fixed their eyes on the youngest Peach. "Sit!"

By some miracle, Dasher and Vix did exactly as they were told. Herb offered each of them a treat from his pocket. Lucy couldn't believe it—Herb had actually managed to train the dogs to do something on command! But before she could be too amazed by this turn of events, Rudy grabbed the bottom of one of Lois's pant legs in his mouth and tugged. Startled by all the commotion, Donny lifted one leg and peed on the shoe that their guest had just taken off beside the back door.

"Bad dogs!" Herb yelled, swiping each of the two misbehaving pups into his arms. "No!" Lucy hustled to grab Lois's shoe—which was, luckily, a strappy sport sandal-type thing that could be easily washed in the sink. Meanwhile, Dad apologized profusely, and Freddy just closed his eyes and moaned.

By this point, Lois was nearly doubled over with laughter.

"I'm so sorry," Dad said again and again. "I don't know what's gotten into them!"

Lucy dragged the other two dogs out of the room by their collars. She followed Herb to the "piano" room (which was really just a sitting room full of fussy furniture and a bunch of stale old books), where they closed the four naughty pups in with a bowl of water and a stern "Behave!"

As soon as the dogs were contained, Herb turned to Lucy with a broad smile. "Did you see how nicely Dasher and Vix sat when I told them to?" he asked proudly. "My training's working!"

Lucy took a deep breath. Though two dogs *sitting* on command was a big accomplishment for these four specific pups, a chewed-on pair of pants and pee in Lois's shoe was not the best official start to their new business. "He peed on her shoe," Lucy muttered.

Herb chewed his lower lip. "Yeah . . . we might want to consider locking the dogs up on the fourth floor when other guests check in, huh? Maybe we can put them in your room, since it's bigger and not as messy and full of stuff as mine."

"That's probably the safest bet," Lucy said.

But even as she tentatively agreed to this plan, Lucy couldn't help thinking about the fact that she really didn't *want* any more living things spending time in her bedroom. For the past week, ever since Herb had convinced himself his dollhouse—and thus the entire *mansion*—was definitely haunted, he'd been sleeping in a little blanket nest on the floor of Lucy's bedroom. Because Herb was almost *always* attached to her (he refused to be anywhere in the house alone, for fear of ghosts), Lucy hadn't gotten more than a few minutes to herself for nearly a week. She hadn't gotten any time to go back up to explore more of the attic, and Herb kept insisting they read extra chapters of *The Vanderbeekers* and more stories from the *Yasmin* chapter books (which Herb was reading for his classroom book club) at night—so Lucy wasn't getting much of her own reading time in, either.

When she and Herb returned to the kitchen, they learned that Dad had already escorted Lois to The Winter Suite. She had told Dad and Freddy that she was eager to take a nap before dinner. "The drive wore her out, I guess," Freddy explained.

As if on cue, the sound of a power saw suddenly echoed through the house. Moments later, the rhythmic and jarring *thud-thud-thud* of a hammer joined in.

Overhead, Lucy could hear the two Handy Gals shouting back and forth to each other over the noise of their tools—in the guest room that was *right* under The Winter Suite. Lucy had gotten so used to the two carpenters being around that she'd actually forgotten they were even in the house that afternoon. But now, they'd made their presence *very* known—to everyone.

Dad's footsteps thudded down the stairs, just as the front doorbell rang with a loud *ding-dong-ding-dong-ding-dong!* Freddy raced out of the kitchen and through the living room and entryway to answer it. A loud, booming voice hollered out, "You called a plumber to take a look at some shower problem? They sent me."

Hearing an unfamiliar voice set the dogs to barking. Stuck inside the front room of the mansion, they yipped and woofed and howled, eager to protect the house from would-be intruders. The noises echoing through the mansion were so loud that they could wake the dead— or, at the very least, a sleepy Lois Sibberson.

"So much for rest and relaxation," Lois said with a yawn, wandering back down into the kitchen. "Got anything good to eat around here, or should I bake us a cake?"

BRAINSTORMING:
Possible new names for The Peach Pit

Peachy Keen B&B

The Peach Throne

Duluth's Best Stay

Comfort to the Core

The Legend of the Three Dawns

The Black Swan

Pigs for Breakfast

Flying Pig Inn

Stone Fruit B&B

Peach Palace

THE PEACH PIT

DAD'S DUTCH BABY PANCAKES

- **2 medium apples**
- **1/4 C sugar**
- **1 C flour**
- **3/4 C sugar**
- **1 C milk**
- **4 eggs**
- **4 T butter**

1. Preheat oven to 425° F.
2. Peel and slice apples and place in a bowl with 1/4 cup sugar.
3. In another bowl, combine the flour and 1/2 cup sugar.
4. Add milk and eggs to flour mixture and whisk until smooth.
5. Heat an iron skillet over medium high heat. Add butter. Once butter is melted, add apples and then pour batter on top.
6. Heat the whole mess on the stove for 1–2 minutes, then put the pan in a preheated oven. Cook for 15 minutes.
7. It should come out all puffy and yummy, and you can serve topped with powdered sugar.

14

SWIM-TIME SOCIAL HOUR

Lois Sibberson's visit was a disaster. Herb had been so excited to welcome his family's very first guest to their new B&B . . . but absolutely everything that could have gone wrong, went wrong.

First came the nap-time construction.

Then, a pipe burst somewhere deep within the walls while Lois was taking a long, hot shower in her guest room bathroom.

Before bed, while Lois was baking a cake for dessert, the dogs somehow managed to slither into Lois's guest room (*How?!* Herb kept wondering), and chewed holes in several of her socks.

The next morning, the oven broke just as Freddy and Dad started making Lois her breakfast. Luckily, it had held out long enough for Lois to make the delicious chocolate cake the previous night, but in the morning they'd had to serve her stale Cheerios, along with home-made scones she pulled out of the freezer in her food truck.

But possibly most embarrassing, Herb had had a horrible nightmare and woke up screaming and sweaty in the middle of the night. Lois had obviously heard him sobbing (she was sleeping in the guest room below them, on the third floor), because she asked if he was feeling better during breakfast the next morning. He'd never felt like such a baby. But ever since Freddy had told him about the creepy noises coming from the wall beside his dollhouse, and ever since things had started mysteriously *moving* inside his mini-mansion during the night, Herb's worries and fears about their house being haunted had returned with gusto.

He hated the Peach Pit once again.

Luckily, his shifts at Birch Pond always cheered him up and gave him a welcome break from the creaky old mansion. Herb had become something of a fixture at the retirement community, and demand for his services was now greater than the time he had available to spend there. Everyone wanted him to come by their apartments to help out with little things, and Herb hated that he'd had to start turning people down. But he couldn't let his new job interfere with his schoolwork or the tasks he'd been asked to do at the Peach Pit (he *loved* helping his dad paint the trim around the outside of the windows and had discovered how much fun it was to wash the glass and see what a big difference a clean window made!). There was only so much one eight-year-old could do in a day's work.

Somehow, Great Aunt Lucinda had convinced the Birch Pond staff to let Herb play in the therapy pool from time to time as a special treat for all his hard work. So after a long, hot shift spent dusting and rearranging books on one resident's bookshelves the Sunday after Lois Sibberson's visit, Herb bounced around in the pool to unwind. Diane and Caroline joined him, water-jogging laps around the edges of the shallow pool. Great Aunt Lucinda popped off that day's curly orangeish-brown wig and strapped on a swim cap that looked a lot like a rubber playground ball. Then she, too, joined them in the water.

"I've got eczema, so I don't do pools unless someone makes me get in for exercise," Joye muttered grouchily, refusing to join in the fun. But she hovered nearby on the pool deck and scowled at them while they swam, making rude faces every time a drop of water came anywhere near her. Herb wanted to suggest she take her bad mood somewhere else and let them have some fun, but he didn't have the nerve.

While he bobbed through the water, nestled inside the snuggly life jacket the staff made him wear while he swam in their pool, Herb told the ladies about Lois Sibberson's disastrous visit and the latest happenings at the Peach Pit.

"I'm pretty sure the Peach Pit is haunted," Herb blurted out, feeling like a goofy goober as soon as he said it out loud.

Great Aunt Lucinda blew tiny bubbles with her nose and mouth as she floated across the surface of the pool. "Why do you think that?" she asked, holding her head all the way out of the water.

Herb noticed she did not disagree with him, nor laugh, nor tell him he was being silly. Any of those responses would have made him feel better. But instead, Great Aunt Lucinda had answered with a question, which made him think that his haunting suspicions were *correct*! "The walls make funny noises," Herb said. "And the stuff inside my dollhouse moves around at night. Like someone—or something—is playing with it while we're all asleep."

"Well, that is creepy," Diane muttered from across the pool.

Herb took a deep breath, accidentally sucking in a little pool water in the process. He coughed and sputtered, his eyes watering from the chlorine or possibly some tears. Diane was an old person; wasn't it her job to make him feel *better*, not worse, about scary stuff?

"I remember I had this doll as a kid that had a real evil look about it," Caroline said, pausing to hook her elbows over the edge of the pool and just float there in the water. "Then one day, that doll up and disappeared. It's like it walked off, all on its own. I still don't know where it went, but boy was I glad it was gone."

Herb's eyes went wide. Usually, he liked kind Caroline . . . but that story wasn't going to help him sleep more soundly at night!

"When I was your age," Diane told Herb, "I was certain that the house on the corner of my block was haunted. There was a light in one of the rooms upstairs that stayed on all night long, and sometimes I'd see a shadow just sitting there in the window."

Herb gulped. "Was it . . . a ghost?"

"Maybe." Diane laughed. "Or maybe it was the writer who lived there. I think he kept odd hours. But still, it creeped me out."

Diane's *maybe* hadn't been reassuring enough to make Herb feel a whole lot better. Maybe it had been some night owl writer, or maybe it *had* been a ghost living in that house. Diane had even admitted that she never knew for sure!

Suddenly, Caroline blurted out, "Do you ladies remember Ouija boards?"

The other three women all tittered and began talking at once. "What's a *wee-jee* board?" Herb asked, even though he was pretty sure he didn't want to know. Even the friendly-looking jack-o'-lantern pumpkin cutouts hanging on the window of the therapy pool room felt suddenly ominous with all this talk of scary stuff and hauntings.

"It's this board game that's been around for years," Diane explained with a laugh. "Supposedly, you can ask questions of the board, and spirits will answer."

"Spirits?" Herb asked, feeling suddenly cold in the usually warm pool. Now he was regretting bringing up his fear that the Peach Pit was haunted. This conversation had not helped at *all*.

Great Aunt Lucinda had finally begun to notice Herb's discomfort. "Ladies, that's enough of that kind of talk," she said.

Joye harrumphed from her poolside perch. "This is all a bunch of nonsense," she said, looking straight at Herb as she stood up. "Your house is not haunted, so don't let them scare you into believing your own silly ideas."

Herb looked at Joye, shocked that *she*, of all people, was the one trying to reassure him. Out of everyone he'd met at Birch Pond, Joye was the last person he'd ever expect to comfort him.

Joye blew her nose into a handkerchief, then tucked the slip of cloth up into the sleeve of her sweater for safekeeping. She leaned against the back of her chair and said, "It's pipes making those noises, and don't ever convince yourself otherwise. Old houses settle and creak and they like to tell their stories—just like all of us old people do. I'll promise you this: If your house is chatting, it means it likes you and is trying to keep you company in the only way it knows how. It's the pipes passing down history, the century-old radiators promising you heat and comfort, or the wood floors and stairs reminding you just how many people have walked and lived and loved in the house before you." Joye stopped talking and glared at him.

Herb got the sense she was waiting for him to respond, but he had nothing to say—so he just nodded at her.

She nodded back. "And if stuff's getting moved inside your dollhouse at night, I'd put my money on your brother or sister. Mark my words on that."

Herb nodded again, then climbed out of the pool and wrapped himself up in a towel.

"Watch yourself," Joye scolded as Herb passed by. "Don't dribble any of that wet on me."

"Sorry," Herb muttered. Then he flashed Joye a smile and said, "And thanks." The way Joye had explained all those creepy old noises the Peach Pit was always making? It made sense. The house was just telling him its stories! That idea made Herb feel a whole lot better. So maybe she wasn't always very friendly, but Joye could obviously be kind when it counted—and that was good enough for Herb.

Joye suddenly shuffled out into the hallway without another word.

"Since when do you have a dollhouse?" Great Aunt Lucinda asked Herb, after the door to the pool had closed behind Joye.

"Lucy found a small version of the Peach Pit in one of the servant staircases," Herb explained, trying to get his mind firmly off board games that talked and dolls that walked and spooky old shadows pacing back and forth in the middle of the night.

Great Aunt Lucinda pulled her eyebrows together. "Did she now?"

"And she gave it to me," Herb said proudly. "As a special present."

"I was wondering where that got tucked away,"

Great Aunt Lucinda said, as much to herself as to Herb. "I remember my David and your dad futzing around with that dollhouse quite a bit back when they were kids. They got really into it for a while. They would set up battles and made little movies using the scenes they created." Herb smiled, thinking this sounded like a very fun idea and planned to try that himself sometime! "One summer they started building some furniture to put inside it and after your dad left to go home, David added some little pieces of printed art to the walls." She smiled at Herb. "Have you noticed it's an almost-exact replica of the big house?"

Herb felt proud that he *had* noticed that. "Yeah," he said. "But I have a question . . ." Herb had been using the dollhouse as a sort of map, exploring all the rooms and hidden staircases of the old house on a small scale, since he was too nervous to explore the *big* version of the *actual* house. But after verifying that almost everything was as it should be in the dollhouse, there was one thing that stumped him. "Why does the dollhouse version of the mansion have an extra layer of rooms on the very bottom? The dollhouse has a giant open space underneath the living room and kitchen and piano room, but I haven't seen a door to a basement or anything. So what's that all about?"

Great Aunt Lucinda nodded. "That's the cellar."

Herb gawped at her. "What's the *cellar*?"

"I used it for storage, mostly," Aunt Lucinda answered. "You'd like it down there—it's full of shelves and old bits and bobs. You should poke around and have a look, see what kinds of fun treasures are tucked away. Maybe you'll find something wonderful hiding down there."

"How do I get to it?" Herb asked, his curiosity piqued.

"You have to go down from the outside of the house. There's an old wooden door nestled into the side of the house behind all those overgrown ferns," Great Aunt Lucinda told him. "Some vines may have grown up over it, since I haven't been down there in years, but it should be pretty easy for you to push those aside and prop the door open."

Herb shivered inside his big, fluffy towel. The idea of poking around in an old, deserted cellar hidden away in the ground under the Peach Pit kind of gave him the willies. But it was also exciting to think that *he* knew about a secret part of the mansion that neither of his siblings nor his dad knew existed. He'd been reading about secret tunnels that were hidden under Duluth's streets; the idea of uncovering his own special space deep underground? That was pretty tempting. This could be Herb's very own corner of the house; a special hideout for Herb and Herb alone. He wouldn't have to share with Dad or Lucy or Freddy, and Herb could decide all by himself exactly what he wanted to do with the space. A hidden room of his own, and no one else would ever need to know about it. "No meatloaf lunch for me today," Herb told the ladies, tugging his pants and sweatshirt on right over his still-wet swimsuit. "I've got to get home."

Thanks to Joye, Herb was feeling a lot less spooked by the house now. And anyway, no amount of fear could keep him from investigating something *this* exciting.

15

SECRETS IN THE WALLS

When Mrs. Fig, Freddy's beloved art teacher, asked him for an update on his piece for the art competition the following week, Freddy was forced to stretch the truth. "It's coming along *great*!" he told her, flashing his most charming smile.

"I'm so happy to hear that," Mrs. Fig said. "When will I get to see something? I'd love to take a look at your progress."

"Oh," Freddy choked out. "Well, it's too big for me to move. There's no way I can get it to school. I'm building it in the shed outside my house. It's *massive*. You'll just have to trust me and be surprised when I drop it off for the show judging."

"Fair enough." Mrs. Fig laughed. "I knew you'd take this opportunity and run with it!"

Freddy laughed along with her, then hustled out of the art classroom beside his friend, Ethan. "What are you building?" Ethan asked.

"Nothing yet," Freddy confessed. "But I have big plans!"

"You told Mrs. Fig it's coming along great," Ethan reminded him.

"Ideas are the important part," Freddy explained with a casual shrug. "And I've got *plenty* of ideas for what I want to build—I just haven't started *implementing* any of them yet." Sort of like his guest room at the B&B, Freddy thought to himself. He had plenty of *ideas* for what he wanted the room to look like—an undersea aquarium, or a medieval fortress, or a room lined with bubble wrap, maybe—but he hadn't actually started the process of decorating it yet. The ideas and planning took time; doing the work would follow . . . eventually. At least, that's what he hoped would happen. But he still hadn't had his breakthrough moment, and Freddy was getting more than a little nervous about where things stood with all the projects on his plate.

With their Thanksgiving deadline to finish the B&B—and the opening of the art competition—now less than a month away, Freddy knew he had to get a move on. The issue was he had always been the kind of guy who most enjoyed sinking into the *process* of building and creating things and couldn't be hurried along if it meant compromising quality. Still, Freddy knew that if his guest room wasn't ready for their grand opening when Dad's cousin David and Great Aunt Lucinda came to stay, they would lose the mansion. And if he didn't finish his piece for the art show, he'd disappoint Mrs. Fig and give up his chance to *win* this important art competition.

He'd get it all done. He had to.

Still, there was that wiggle of worry again. Something tickling at his confidence, making him nervous: *What if I don't finish it all?* Freddy had *so much* going on, and not enough time to get it all done. At least, not well. Unless lightning struck, and struck soon.

"Did you know people used to use horsehair and old newspapers to insulate their houses?" Freddy asked Ethan, quickly changing topics. There wasn't much sense in dwelling on what he hadn't yet done; he could worry and fret constantly, but that wasn't going to actually get his stuff built. He'd just have to really work hard over the next few weeks and make serious progress. That moment of inspiration would come. But would the breakthrough moment come in *time*? "The Handy Gals—those are the two college kids that are helping us fix up the house—are knocking out a wall in Herb and Dad's guest room today, and I can't wait to see what they find inside. I hope it's filled with horsehair."

"Can I come over?" Ethan asked. "Think they'd let *me* help knock the wall down?"

"Yeah, for sure," Freddy replied. "They're pretty cool. I hang out nearby every time one of them comes in with a sledgehammer, since that usually means something epic is about to happen. Kassy let me try out her nail gun yesterday. Dad looked like he was going to have a heart attack when he came into the room and saw me holding it. I guess he almost shot a nail through his own foot one time, so he gets a little weird about nail guns. He's more a *pie* guy than a *tool* guy."

After dismissal, Freddy met up with Ethan and Henry outside the side door closest to the fifth-grade classrooms. The weather was already getting very cold—Duluth was so far north in Minnesota that it often snowed before Halloween—so the season of biking to and from school wouldn't last much longer. Freddy loved the freedom that came with biking places, and he dreaded the months when he had to take the bus home with all the little kids, like Herb. So until then, Freddy was going to take advantage of whatever bike-to-school days were left. Both of his best friends lived near Freddy's old house, but they often biked home with him after school to check out the progress on the Peach Pit and investigate whatever disaster was under construction that day.

When they got to the house, Freddy popped a frozen pizza into the new oven and let his friends roam around. Ethan and Henry were both obsessed with exploring the servant staircases and loved playing a game they called "Spoiled Rich Guy" using the house's intercom system. They all split up into different rooms and took turns being the most obnoxious Spoiled Rich Guy imaginable.

"Hellooooo?" Ethan called to Freddy and Henry through the intercom from one of the under-construction second-floor bedrooms. In a funny accent, he said, "I demand that you bring me fourteen green M&Ms and thirty-two pink Starburst. I like my Starburst to be cut in half, and they must be *out* of the wrappers. But don't touch them with your filthy hands, Bertholomew! Chop chop! You have two minutes, or you're FIRED!"

Giggling, Freddy took the next turn playing the part of Spoiled Rich Guy. "Willard! Willard, my trusty butler, are you there?" he barked into the intercom. "My pillow has gotten flat under my face, and I need you to flip it. You know I don't like when my face has to touch the warm side of the pillow!"

Next, Henry got a turn. He raced down to the kitchen and yelped into the intercom, "I spilled my milk, Clark. It's all over the floor, and it's all your fault, Clark! Come down here and clean it up this *instant*!"

Their roleplaying game kept them all busy until the pizza was ready. While they ate, sloppily and standing up over plates that never actually got used except to catch sauce drips, Freddy showed his friends some of the projects he'd gotten to be a part of during the house's construction. "I put on that doorknob . . . and that one. YouTube taught me everything I needed to know! Then I helped paint this room, and in here, I was in charge of emptying a bucket all night when the sink upstairs started leaking through the ceiling."

Just as they were loading their pizza plates into the Peach Pit's ancient dishwasher, Herb came strolling through the back door. He was chatting away with the Handy Gals, Kassy and Lila. The two carpenters-slash-fix-it-people were each carrying sledgehammers and had plastic goggles perched on their foreheads.

"Who's ready to break stuff?" Lila asked the group gathered in the kitchen.

Freddy had never seen his two best friends so eager and willing to work. While Herb settled in at the dining room table with his Tiny Genius math homework,

Henry and Ethan both jumped up and chased after Kassy and Lila, giggling excitedly at the prospect of knocking down a wall. Each of the Peach kids had their own pair of safety goggles, so Freddy passed Lucy's to Henry and Herb's to Ethan, and the three boys waited for their instructions.

"We need to break through this wall between the closet and the bedroom because there's probably some serious rot going on, thanks to a pipe that broke in the ceiling above it sometime a few decades ago," Kassy explained. "The plumber discovered a few major issues that no one's dealt with, and it's time to see what's hiding up in there. So we're gonna knock this wall out and get rid of the closet, which will make this guest room a little bigger. Breaking stuff is the best part of my job."

Lila held her sledgehammer toward Ethan, who looked as excited as he did after finding a hidden relic or being bequeathed a special royal sword at Cardboard Camp. Ethan staggered under the weight of the giant tool but managed to draw it back far enough to get a weak, pendulum-like swing at the wall. The head of the sledgehammer barely kissed the old plaster before landing on the floor with a *thud*.

"You gotta swing it like you mean it," Kassy told him. "Pretend you're a lumberjack swinging an ax at a tree, or that you're some sort of knight in medieval times who needs to slay a dragon."

"*Now* you're speaking my language," Ethan said. He grunted and let the weight of the sledgehammer drag him backward. With another mighty grunt, he swayed forward and let the head of the sledgehammer pound against the wall. It thwacked and let out a satisfying *boom*, but didn't even make a crack in the solid wall. Henry and Freddy each took a couple turns, but still the wall didn't budge. "It's like trying to break a piñata," Freddy growled. "Hopefully, there's candy inside when we finally get it open."

Lila took a look at her watch and wiggled her fingers to get them to hand over the sledgehammer. "This is obviously woman's work," she said with a smirk, then heaved the giant sledgehammer over her shoulder and swung at the wall, immediately breaking through the hundred-year-old plaster. The wall split open with a *crack*.

Freddy and his friends cheered as Lila took swing after swing at the wall, splitting it open a little more with every hit. Once she'd knocked past the layers of wallpaper and broke all the way through, it was easier to knock out pieces of the wall with every swing. So she gave each of the boys a few more turns until they were all sweaty and weary and sore. The wall came down in chunks and crumbles, with plaster flying everywhere— getting in their hair and their ears and all over their clothes. After a while, Herb came up to watch and over- see the work; it was *his* guest room getting destroyed, after all. He clasped his hands over his ears to block out the noise of each swing.

"Hold on," Freddy said, jumping up just after Kassy had taken a huge chunk out of the bottom right cor- ner of the wall. The divider between the closet and the bedroom was almost gone, leaving a gaping hole that hadn't been there half an hour before. "What's that?"

Ethan and Henry both scuttled forward to join him. Herb was close on their heels. Freddy poked at the rub- ble with his shoe, moving aside chunks of dusty plaster. There, tucked inside one of the walls of the Peach Pit, was a very old, very dusty, very *creepy* doll's head.

"What the—" Freddy's eyes went wide as he backed away from the tiny face staring back at him from inside the wall. He'd been messing with Herb for the past cou- ple weeks, moving stuff around in the dollhouse at night to try to convince his brother that the mansion was haunted. But maybe Freddy had been closer to the truth than he'd thought—maybe the mansion *was* haunted, and it was because this baby doll had been stuck—and *angry!*—inside the walls of their house for a hundred years.

Suddenly, a tiny squeak echoed out of the hole in the wall.

"It's talking to us!" Ethan screamed, scrambling backward.

"I'm out of here," Henry said, bolting from the room.

Freddy wasn't as quick to react. But he jumped up from his crouch when, seconds later, something alive squirmed out of the now-open wall and raced across the room. Herb squealed with delight. "Mousey!" he called out.

Freddy backed away, feeling sick, guilty, and terrified. He was *sick* about the fact that he'd just gotten concrete proof that there were mice living within the walls of his house. And he felt *guilty* that he had been teasing Herb about his fear of creepy noises in the walls, and now one of *Freddy's* worst fears had just popped out to spook him. But more than anything, he was *terrified* about how, why, and when this doll head had taken up residence inside the wall of the house. Who had put it there?

Freddy was spooked, which meant his brother must be terrified. A ghostly doll head nestled inside the bedroom wall? *Yeesh!* This was the stuff of nightmares.

But when Freddy turned around to see how Herb was handling this turn of events, he noticed his brother was actually creeping *toward* the wall. Herb squatted down and brought his face level with the dusty doll head. He reached inside the pile of debris and picked up the head with one hand. "Well, hello," Herb said, greeting it royally. "You look like you've lived here for a while. What's your story?"

WHAT CAN YOU GROW
OUT OF A PEACH PIT?

FREDDY'S TREEHOUSE
"Construction Room"

Bird's Nest

Clarissa's High-
Quality Nails

Hammers

Beehive
(ouch)

Nails

Wooden Planks

Pile of
Gold Coins

Bricks

Stacks
of Cash

16

THE KEY TO THE MAP

In the week leading up to Halloween, several disastrous things happened.

First, Lucy got a B on one of her Language Arts essays. Lucy had never gotten a B on *anything* before, and certainly not on an essay about a book she'd read and loved and had many thoughts about. But there it was, glaring back at her from the student portal up on the monitor of the family's desktop computer: failure.

Next, all four of the dogs got covered in burrs. For some reason, Herb had been tromping and poking around in the ferns and overgrown vines that lined the outer edge of the mansion, and the dogs had all followed him into the mess of greenery and weeds one afternoon. They'd come out with their belly fur absolutely coated in pokey burrs that nestled into all the soft hair in their leg pits and bellies. It took Lucy and Herb *two whole days* to pluck them all off, and still they'd had to cut off some fur to get the little rugrats totally burr-free.

Then, Freddy and Herb had discovered a decapitated doll's head and a bunch of mice inside one of the walls of the mansion. Freddy had described the discovery as something "like a piñata!" The boys and Freddy's friends had been helping the Handy Gals knock open a wall, and instead of candy falling out when they broke it open, the walls of the house had spit out a mysterious doll head and vermin. *Awesome.*

But worst of all was Dad's cousin David. When Lucy got home from school one afternoon, she found a truck parked on the street outside the house with the words BAKSHI BROTHERS WINDOWS written in big, bright letters on the side. There was a whole crew of workers installing fresh new windows in most rooms of the mansion. "What are you doing?" Lucy called out, trying to sound like someone in charge. But with a whole flock of workers strutting to and fro, it was hard to get anyone's attention. "Hello?"

A big, burly guy sporting a flannel shirt strolled over and said, "Looking a lot better, eh? We should be done this afternoon. I brought my whole crew out to get it done quick for you."

"We—" Lucy began. "We didn't order windows." Suddenly, Lucy worried that maybe her dad *had* ordered windows. But windows were expensive, she'd learned, and she knew their pot of money was dwindling much faster than repairs were getting done on the house. Unless he'd stumbled upon a winning lottery ticket that she didn't know about, there was no way Dad could afford this many fancy new windows.

The guy glanced down at a clipboard in his enormous left hand. "David Peach? Is that your dad?"

"David Peach . . ." Lucy muttered. What was Dad's cousin *David* doing ordering windows for the house?

She got her answer that night when David called to talk through what *he* referred to as "all this bed-and-breakfast insanity" with Dad. Her dad got off the phone with his cousin, whom he hadn't spoken to in years, and was obviously far more flustered than usual. "He's convinced this whole plan of Lucinda's is a terrible idea," Dad explained to Lucy in private that night. "He doesn't think this house should or ever *could* be a B and B, and he's very concerned about Aunt Lucinda's money situation. He strongly believes she ought to sell this house, so he ordered new windows to help improve its value. He has a potential buyer coming by to look at the place with their Realtor tomorrow, and there's an appraiser stopping by next week to figure out what a good price would be."

"What's an appraiser?" Lucy asked.

"Someone who looks at all the details of a house and decides what its value is. They look at things like numbers of bedrooms, the quality of the bathrooms and kitchen, what condition the house is in, repairs and renovations that have been done, and how much similar houses have sold for in this area recently."

"B-but," Lucy stammered. "But it's not even Thanksgiving. He can't decide this until we've been given our fair shot."

"He's trying to get the ball rolling so things will move quickly come December," Dad said with a sigh. "And he offered to pay us back for all the money we've spent on improvements, if and when he does sell the house. He admitted it wouldn't be fair for us to spend money sprucing the place up and not get something in return."

"But . . ." Lucy didn't even know what to say. "But we live here. Aunt Lucinda wants us to keep the house in the family. She *wants* us to be here!"

"We've always known this could be temporary," Dad reminded her. He looked around at the piles of lumber, and sheetrock, and half-empty cans of paint that seemed to multiply around them every single day. Several dogs came trotting into the room, and Lucy noticed that Vix's paw was *still* blue from the day she'd grabbed a paint-filled paintbrush in her mouth and run laps around the Peach Pit.

Dad shook his head and flopped against the back of a living room chair. He was cradling Mom's favorite throw pillow in his arms, hugging it tight like it was some sort of life raft. "My cousin might be right. I don't know if we can actually do this, Lulu," Dad admitted. "Maybe they should just sell the house, and we could give up on this insanity."

"We're making good progress," Lucy insisted, though she wasn't sure this was true. It felt like there was always more to do, and everything they finished led to yet another project. Lucy didn't have enough time to focus on her homework, Dad's bald spot was expanding, Freddy was hardly making any progress on his art project for the competition he'd been so excited about, and Herb had started having full-on conversations with the dogs. They were all going a little crazy. If it weren't for the Handy Gals keeping everything running along, the house would likely have fallen down by now. But she loved this house and hated that Dad's cousin had poisoned him into thinking the latest Great Peach

Experiment was a crazy idea. Maybe it was, but Aunt Lucinda's logic made sense to *Lucy*. "We can't give up. I mean, we've spent all the rest of Mom's money and lots of our time making really important improvements, and we have one and a half guest rooms ready, so it's not like we're back at square one. We just need to make sure everything is perfect before David gets here, and then he'll see that we belong in this house and Aunt Lucinda made the right choice when she gave it to us to take care of for her. She wanted to keep it in the family, remember?"

Saying this out loud didn't convince Lucy they were anywhere *close* to ready, but it did remind her how much she wanted to hold on to the Peach Pit. This was a new, permanent home for their family; a place for them to rebuild and grow as a family of four and make new memories. She loved her room, she loved her hide-away attic space, she loved the hidden staircases, and she loved dreaming about how many interesting people they would get to meet and talk to when they opened the B&B to guests. But most of all, there was just so much family history in this place, so how could anyone even consider letting it go?

"Remember what Mom always used to say?" Lucy muttered quietly, as much to herself as to her dad. "If you

want to build something incredible, you have to keep trying, even when everything seems like it's falling apart."

"But Lulu," Dad said, resting his chin on Mom's pillow, "this house is *actually* falling apart. I don't think
your mom meant that quite so literally."

The next night, Lucy finished up her homework as
quickly as possible. She wanted some time to sneak up
to the attic to keep exploring. But first, she headed into
Herb's room to tuck him in for the night. He'd finally
stopped sleeping in her room, though she wasn't really
sure what had changed to convince him it was time for
him to move back into his own room. They hadn't solved
the mystery of what was making noises in the walls by
Herb's dollhouse (and Lucy hadn't actually *heard* these
noises with her own two ears—so she was still pretty
sure that was a story made up by Freddy, just to spook
Herb), but Herb just didn't seem bothered by the haunted
sounds anymore. In fact, it was almost right after they'd
found the mice and doll head living in the wall that he
seemed to turn a corner.

Herb was now endlessly fascinated by the history of
their old house, and had checked out a bunch of books
about Duluth history from the public library. He'd
started spouting off facts about their hometown almost
as frequently as Freddy blurted out *his* random facts.

"Did you know there's a whole network of secret tunnels underground that run through the city?" he asked one day. "Did you know Duluth was once home to more millionaires, per capita, than any other city in the world? The whole *world*!"

Sometimes, Lucy decided, it felt like she lived on a shelf full of encyclopedias. Her brothers—and her dad, for that matter—were chock-full of unlimited information about almost any topic.

When she got to Herb's room that night, she found him sitting in the middle of his bedroom floor surrounded by scraps of paper and stamps and stickers and markers. He was obviously *art*-ing, and Lucy felt bad for interrupting him to tell him it was time to go to sleep. "What'cha making?" she asked, settling in beside him.

"An invitation," Herb replied, tongue poking out the corner of his mouth, the way it did when he was really concentrating.

"For what?"

"A fancy tea party," Herb explained.

"Where?" Lucy asked. "Here?"

Herb looked up at her. "Yeah, you know my teacher, Mr. Andrus? He does a Mother-Son Tea at school every year, and I can't go. So I'm making my own tea party. You'll be invited, and my stuffies, and Aunt Lucinda, and Diane and Caroline, and even mean Joye."

Lucy shook her head and laughed. "Hold on. First of all, who are Diane and Caroline and mean Joye? Are those girls in your class?"

"They're Great Aunt Lucinda's friends. And mine, too. I work for them at Birch Pond."

Lucy laughed again. "You *work* for them?"

Herb then launched into a story about how he'd picked up a job at the Birch Pond retirement community and told Lucy he'd been going there several times each week to help out. "You're all busy with your guest rooms here, so I figured I'd keep myself busy, too. They pay well."

"You get *paid*?" Lucy balked.

"I get paid in tips, and lunch, and on long days, I earn the right to swim in their pool." Herb thrust out his chin. "I'm very good at my job."

"Does Dad know about this?" Lucy asked.

Herb shrugged. "Sure. He even signed the permission slip for me to swim in the therapy pool. Aunt Lucinda must have talked to him about the job, because then he asked me about it, and he told me it was okay."

"Oh, Herb," Lucy said, laughing still. "You are the best." As she flopped back on the striped rug that covered most of Herb's bedroom floor, she thought about how nice it was to see her dad *parenting* again. After their mom died, Lucy had taken up a lot of the responsibility for her brothers. But now, Dad was back in the driver's seat . . . sometimes, anyway. "Now, what's this about a tea party?" She lowered her voice and looked at him steadily. "A Mother-Son Tea?"

"But I don't have a mom," Herb said. "Aunt Lucinda and her friends told me there must be some sort of work-around, so that's what I'm trying to figure out. I decided to host my *own* tea party, and you can come even if you don't have a mom anymore. It's for anyone."

Lucy squeezed her lips into a thin line. "You can't be the only boy in class without a mom," Lucy said grimly. "Mr. Andrus has to understand that."

You're Invited!
To Herb's Tea Party

Tell your family!

You don't need a mom to come to this tea party!

Tell your friends!

This is a party you can't miss!

When: 11:00 am Nov 23
Where: The Peach Pit
What: Herb's Tea Party
Who: Anyone who loves a good time!

Herb shrugged and bowed his head over his glue stick and purple construction paper. "I dunno. But can we not talk about it? I'm working around it, so it's fine."

Lucy wanted to respect her brother's wishes, so she dropped it—for now. But she was going to get to the bottom of this. A mother-son tea party was a very outdated concept. What about the kids with two dads? Or the kids who lived with grandparents, or aunts, or a single dad, or a family friend? So far, she'd liked almost everything Herb had told her about his third-grade teacher, but not this. This made her angry.

As soon as Lucy had tucked Herb in and nestled her stuffed duck next to his pig for company, she returned to her room. To block out her frustration about Mr. Andrus's Mother-Son Tea, Lucy climbed up to the attic. She'd dragged a lamp up there, and had woven an extension cord through the closet to plug it in, since the attic was pretty dark and creepy at night.

Over the past few weeks, Lucy had made it most of the way through the boxes. She'd studied the photographs at length, and poked around in most of the piles of stuff. But there was one deep back corner left for her to explore, and tonight was the night.

As soon as she was safely settled into her secret attic space, with the lamp *on* for safety, Lucy dragged a teetering pile of thick-cardboard boxes out of the spot where she'd first found the dollhouse and into her investigation station. A long, silent bug with about 230 extra legs scuttled out from behind the pile, and Lucy choked back a scream. She peered into the shadows, checking to be sure there wasn't a nest full of many-legged beasts waiting to attack. And that's when she saw it: a small wooden box, nearly hidden between two roof boards. She grabbed it and brought it toward the light. Inside the box was a folded-up piece of paper. She eagerly spread out the crinkled and yellowed paper.

It was covered in a bunch of rough sketches that almost made it look like it might be some kind of map. The pencil writing was *very* faded, and the collection of boxes and lines on the paper didn't make a lot of sense. At first, Lucy couldn't make out much of what was written down. But on closer inspection, she was finally able to read a few numbers on the page, along with the words scrawled at the top of the paper: *The Hunt for Hidden Riches.*

"Hidden riches?" Lucy muttered aloud. She grinned and flopped back against some boxes, then she began to laugh. "How much more stuff is this house hiding?"

The word *Hunt* definitely suggested this was some kind of map. But a map to *what*, and a map of *where*, were the big questions. It just looked like squares inside of squares with some numbers and a bunch of dotted lines twisting around in a messy squiggle.

It was nearly eleven o'clock, but Lucy knew she just *had* to sneak downstairs to get a better look at this mysterious piece of paper. The lighting in her room wasn't great ever since the electrician shut off power to half of her room to do upgrades to their electrical panel. And the attic lamp was dim at best. Lucy needed the big reading lamp in the living room, and maybe a pair of Dad's reading glasses for this job.

One of the dogs, Rudy, pitter-pattered behind her as she crept down the servant stairs from her fourth-floor bedroom. Though it was creepy in the dark, twisty, hidden staircases so late at night, it was safer than trying to sneak down the center staircase without someone hearing. Rudy trotted quietly along behind, for once not barking to alert the whole pack to his whereabouts. Lucy leaned down and rubbed the soft fur between his ears, silently thanking him for not ruining her nighttime sneakery.

Lucy and Rudy popped out of the servant staircase directly into the kitchen. Her dad kept pairs of reading glasses scattered all over the house—on the dining room table to read the paper in the morning, in the living room for when he was reading science journals at night, and in the kitchen to read labels and recipes. It took less than a minute of hunting around for her to find a pair. She slid them on and headed into the living room to flick on the brightest lamp in the house, the one next to the smooshy chair. Rudy hopped up beside her and curled in against her leg. Lucy was glad to have the company, since wandering around the giant mansion all alone at night really was kind of terrifying. She was excited to think about the future, when the B&B would be filled with guests and stories and the laughter of family, friends, and strangers.

As Lucy studied the paper through her dad's powerful reading glasses, the faded lines began to come more into focus. It was still hard to make much out, but with the help of Dad's glasses and in the direct lamplight, Lucy could see things a little more clearly. She squinted, letting her eyes go soft as she considered the shape of the map's lines and boxes. She stared at it for ages, but it didn't make any sense at all. "'The Hunt for Hidden Riches,'" she repeated, reading it off the top of the paper. She stared even harder, desperately trying to make out what all the numbers and shapes might mean.

"Oh!" Lucy gasped suddenly. Rudy jumped up, startled. Lucy wrapped her arms around his skinny little body and nuzzled her face into his fur. "Rudy, do you know what I think this is? It's a map of the Peach Pit!"

THE HUNT FOR HIDDEN RICHES
1
6
4
11
2
5
12
10
FOLLOW THE HUNT FOR HIDDEN RICHES TO

17

UNDERGROUND TURF

It didn't take too much searching before Herb found the warped old door that led down into the Peach Pit's hidden cellar. The door was, as Great Aunt Lucinda had promised, tucked among a thick tangle of vines on one side of the house. Herb had brought his pack of dogs along with him to search for it among the weeds and vines, but quickly learned that there were dozens of patches of burrs buried in the overgrown garden, and they stuck to the dogs' fur like Velcro. After he and Lucy spent hours pulling the burrs out of their fur, Herb accepted the fact that he couldn't keep bringing his whole pack along with him to visit the cellar.

So Herb had chosen Dasher (the best behaved of the dogs) to join him on his next trek into the thick brambles. Dasher trotted along, sticking close beside Herb on a leash. He was the only one of the pack of four that didn't fight the leash like it was some sort of evil villain. His good behavior had earned him the right to join Herb on his field trips to investigate the hidden basement.

The first time Herb opened the cellar door, he'd just peeked inside. Dust covered the stairs leading down into the creepy space, and there were dead moths and bugs everywhere. It smelled damp, and the air that slithered up and out of the space below felt stale and cold.

The second time he snuck around the side of the house to explore the hidden space, he brought a flashlight. He and Dasher opened the door and crept down a few steps to see what they could see. The answer was: not much. More dead bugs and far too much dark silence.

But today, on his third visit to the secret cellar door, Herb had promised himself he would muster up the nerve to creep down the creaky old stairs and enter the cave-like space. He pulled Dasher up into his arms, holding him against his chest like a tiny coat of arms, and stepped carefully onto the top step down. He'd found a headlamp in some of Great Aunt Lucinda's old camping stuff (things she'd loaned to Herb's family after Mom died, which they had never gotten a chance to use), so he had his hands free to carry Dasher close against him as he made his way down, down, down.

At the bottom of the steps, he paused and swiveled his head to get a good look around. The ceilings were low—the space was probably only about as tall as Lucy—and found it was much more magnificent inside the musty old cellar than he ever could have imagined.

The walls were solid and cobwebbed and windowless, and the floors uneven. But the hidden space under the mansion was *huge*. There were dirty wooden shelves lined up all along the outside edges of the room, most of which were empty. It was like a giant treasure chest, just waiting for Herb to fill it with his trinkets and collections!

Lately, Herb had been much less scared about all the spooky stuff that used to make him nervous about the Peach Pit. Really, things had been so much better ever since Joye had pointed out that all the funny noises he kept hearing were just the house telling its story. So now, feeling confident and only a teensy bit creeped out, Herb plopped Dasher down onto the floor and let go of his leash. The skittish pup didn't go far, but he sniffed back into some corners to check things out—and to take a quick pee. "Dash!" Herb scolded.

But then he realized a little bit of dog pee wasn't really going to change the way the musty old cellar smelled. It wasn't as if the space was *clean* or anything. Dasher was just doing what he had to do, and also marking his turf in the process. Herb giggled, thinking about what would happen if *he* marked his turf and *he* peed in a corner of the basement, too. That's something Freddy would do, but not Herb.

Herb wandered through the dark and dusty space, using the thin beam of yellow from his headlamp to light the way. There were mysterious glass jars lined up on one set of shelves, and some old yard furniture was shoved into a back corner. A few dirty tarps were crumpled up on another shelf, along with a bunch of tools and a giant box of rusty-looking nails.

Way at the back of the cellar, along the outer wall, Herb found a small, creaky door built into the concrete foundation of the house. Herb had noticed this door inside the bottommost level of the miniature dollhouse version of the Peach Pit. The dollhouse was proving, time and again, to be a perfect, tiny model of the house itself—almost no details were missing. It was pretty spectacular, actually. Herb was surprised Freddy wasn't more impressed with the dollhouse, especially since he loved building things like that himself. But he was so caught up in working on his art project and his room in the B&B that Herb figured he just didn't have time to be impressed by something of Herb's.

Dasher nosed into the door's opening, so Herb felt like he ought to follow. Herb let Dash lead the way.

What was behind the door? Was it a closet? A door to a hidden world, like Narnia? Herb held the dog's leash tight, even though he knew Dasher wouldn't go far. It made him feel like he was connected to something real, even as he eased open this mysterious door to *something.*

With a loud grunt that echoed through the entire cellar, Herb pushed the door all the way open and peeked inside. Darkness stretched out in front of him—for what could have been ten feet or ten miles. The space behind the door seemed endless. Herb's light only reached a little way into the space, then faded into more darkness. "It kind of looks like a tunnel," Herb whispered. Could this be part of the system of hidden tunnels that snaked under Duluth's city streets? Had Herb just discovered a huge secret about the Peach Pit that no one else knew?

Dasher whined, tucking himself between Herb's legs.

Herb stretched his neck out, trying to make the headlamp's light reach farther for a better view. But even after taking a few steps past the strange door, his light couldn't find the end of the room or tunnel or whatever this space was.

"Do you want to keep going?" Herb asked Dasher. Dasher did not respond, which Herb took as a *no.* The whole cellar was filled with possibilities and interesting stuff and plenty of room to explore. There was no reason

Herb had to go any farther past this strange door and risk getting sucked into a make-believe world or some horrible nether portal. The cellar itself was enough for him.

So he closed the door behind himself and continued to poke around in his secret world under the Peach Pit.

After a while, the headlamp started to flicker. Herb knew he couldn't spend much more time in the basement today, unless he wanted to be stranded in total darkness down here (which he most certainly did not). But before he headed back up the stairs and out into the yard, he took a mental picture of the cellar, so he could make a map to study later. Freddy always said sketching shook his ideas loose, and Herb wanted to spend some time thinking about all the fun ways he could use this newfound secret space! If he wasn't allowed to decorate a room of his own in the B&B, he would adopt *this* room as his own personal fortress.

Just as he was about to step onto the bottom step to climb back out of the ground, Herb heard a familiar squeak from the dark space under the stairs. He'd know the sound of mice anywhere! He grinned, squatted down, and aimed his fading beam of light into the crack between the bottom and second step. Sure enough, there were several pairs of eyes looking back at him. But as soon as the light caught them, the little critters scattered into the darkness beyond. Dasher barked but didn't chase after them.

"Those are our new tiny friends, Dash," Herb explained to the dog. Dasher looked up at him, appearing to both understand and trust what Herb was telling him. "And you know what's great about having those little mouse friends down here?" Herb rubbed his hands together when he realized this. "Even if he found the door to the cellar, Freddy's never going to risk coming down here—he's terrified of mice. So this space? It's *all* ours."

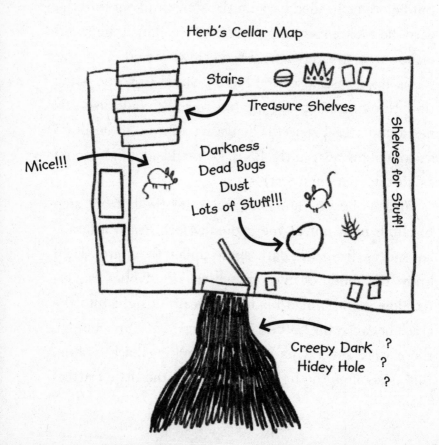

Herb's Cellar Map

18

BUILDING BLUNDERS

Halloween had come and gone, and with November now in full swing, the deadline to finish the Peach Pit B&B and his art show project were both too close for Freddy's comfort. David Peach's wannabe buyers and money people and those real estate nosy nellies kept poking around the mansion, reminding the family of their looming deadline to finish all the work they had left to do.

On top of that, Mrs. Fig kept checking in with Freddy to see how things were going with his build for the art show. Her constant asking did nothing but remind him over and over again that he wasn't nearly as far along as he wanted or needed to be. If he were being totally honest, Freddy would have to admit that nothing about the piece was clicking yet. The project just didn't feel *right* and he hadn't really started building anything at all. He had all the sketches and designs and ideas for his giant dream treehouse drawn up on paper, but now that it was very much time for him to start building it, he hadn't yet found a way to make it feel *special* or uniquely *Freddy*.

And the guest room he was responsible for designing and putting together in the B&B? Well, he still had some serious work to do. Like, *all* the work.

The rest of the house was coming along—slowly. All the new windows were in (thanks to David Peach), the trim had been touched up (with no thanks to the dogs for their extra help), and the roof deemed "acceptable for now." The holes in the mansion's siding had been patched—roughly—and now all attention had shifted to the guts of the house. While Theo—their new employee, the guy helping get some of the details set up for the business side of the B&B—worked on putting together a website (something Freddy had *begged* to do, but reluctantly agreed to pass off to Theo when he realized how many other things were on his to-do list), everyone else tried to finish up all the projects that were half done inside the house.

There were bathrooms torn apart, two of the guest rooms were still in total disrepair, and the living room furniture had all been moved—again—to one side of the room so a chimney guy could deal with some sort of issue that made it so they couldn't light fires in the ancient living room fireplace. (The chimney guy had said something about the fireplace having the flu, which Freddy planned to investigate further.)

Around the first weekend in November, things at the Peach Pit were definitely going not so well . . . and then the buzzing started. It wasn't until Freddy had started spending more time in his guest room that he noticed there was always an unusual humming sound coming from somewhere in the walls. At first, he chalked it up to the ghosts in the walls . . . or just noisy pipes. But then one day, when he was sitting with his eyes closed in the middle of The Freddy Suite, hoping some sort of design inspiration might strike for his guest room plan, Freddy realized the noise coming from inside the wall of his guest room was different from anything he'd heard before.

"Kassy!" he hollered, calling to one of the Handy Gals. She'd been working on repairing a broken hand-rail that was dangerously close to falling off the wall and clattering down the stairs to the next landing down.

"Yo!" Kassy replied.

"Come here, please," Freddy shouted.

A few long minutes later, a very filthy and exhausted-looking Handy Gal came strolling up the central staircase to Freddy's guest room. "What's up?"

"Listen," Freddy said, pointing at the exterior wall.

He and Kassy both stood there, totally silent, listening to the high-pitched buzz coming from inside the wall. "What the heck is that?" Kassy asked.

"I was hoping you would know," Freddy admitted.

"That's not right," Kassy blurted out.

Freddy cringed. "And *that's* not reassuring."

"I think we need to break in and see what's up." Kassy texted Lila, who'd been working downstairs but appeared not long after with a sledgehammer and a flashlight. Herb, Lucy, and Dad were close on her heels. "Just a little hole, to scope things out," Kassy promised.

And then she started whacking away at yet *another* wall in the Peach Pit. This time, it was different from the day they'd discovered the doll's head deep within the walls. Because of the funny noise coming from within, and to minimize the damage, Kassy wanted to be pretty specific with their wall-busting. So all the Peaches stepped back, stood by the door to Freddy's suite, and let the Handy Gals do their thing.

It only took a few well-aimed swings of her hammer before a chunk of plaster crumbled inward, leaving a hole in the wall the size of a bagel. Lila moved her flashlight toward the wall . . . and that's when a slow, drowsy bee came spiraling out. That first bee was quickly followed by a second, a third, and within just a few seconds, a whole river of bees was lazily pouring out of the wall. "I think we found the source of the noise," Freddy blurted out.

The Peaches and the Handy Gals raced to get out the door of Freddy's guest room. Lila was pulling up the rear of the group, and she yelped when one of the bees stung her. "Move it!" she shouted. "They're confused, but they won't be for long!"

Within fifteen seconds, they'd all cleared out of the room. Lucy quickly grabbed a towel from the neighboring suite's bathroom to plug up the space under the bee-room door. "That should keep them inside," she said, using her knees to push the fabric tight against the base of the door.

"Huh," Freddy said. "I'm kinda thinking that's not going to be a very comfortable room for our guests."

Everyone cracked up.

"What are we supposed to do now?" Dad asked, looking absolutely bewildered.

"There are people who handle this sort of thing," Freddy said.

"Like . . . people who kill the bees?" Herb asked, his lip quivering. "We can't hurt them. It's not *their* fault we stole their house. They were here first."

Freddy shook his head. "No, bees are good for the planet, so we definitely don't want to kill them." Herb nodded his agreement as Freddy went on. "I read a story about this lady—a special bee lady—who got called into this house whose walls had been totally overtaken by bees. Like, the insides of her walls were one hundred percent hive. She put on this special suit, and somehow she took apart the hive and moved it in pieces to outside somewhere. She somehow found the queen bee—which, did you know, is usually the mom of almost *all* the other bees inside the hive?!— and moved her, and all her little bee minions followed. I can't remember the specifics of how it all went down, but we could call that lady."

"Where was she located?" Lila asked.

"New Hampshire, maybe?" Freddy guessed. "Or it could have been Maine?"

"Okay," Dad said with a huge sigh. "That's not realistic. But maybe we can find our own bee lady here in Minnesota."

"It's not gonna be cheap," Freddy said softly. "This is, like, high-tech specialty work. And dangerous, probably, too." He grinned. "If you buy me a bee suit, maybe I could do it."

"No!" Dad, Lucy, and Herb all shouted at the same time.

Freddy shrugged. "Okay, let me do some digging and see what we can find out."

"I'll help," Kassy offered. "I'm the one who decided to crack into the bees' house—I sort of feel like it's the least I can do to make up for disturbing their peaceful home."

Freddy high-fived her. "Operation: B and B Bee is underway."

■ ■ ■

A few hours later, Freddy decided it was time to call a family meeting. Over the past few weeks, the Peach Pit "family" had officially grown to include Theo and the two Handy Gals. Freddy convinced Dad to order a couple giant pizzas from everyone's favorite—Sammy's Pizza—to feed the whole crew while he broke the bad news he'd learned about bee removal service. He also thought they ought to talk through where all their other B&B projects stood.

"First of all, bee relocation is definitely *not* cheap," Freddy said through a mouthful of gooey Sammy's Special. It was his favorite kind of pizza—green pepper and onion, topped off with one perfect, round ball of sausage on every piece. Perfection! "Frankly, moving one wall of bees costs more than it would cost to hire movers to move *us* out. Let's just say, we might want to consider an alternative."

"What sort of alternative?" Theo asked. Then he said, "Here's an idea: What if we replaced the plaster wall with clear plexiglass and left the hive inside the wall? Then guests could watch the bees at work. It would actually be really fascinating, and I bet we could get some pretty good publicity with a guest room that has an actual working hive visible through the wall."

Freddy's mouth dropped open and half a sausage ball rolled out. "You are a genius," he said. Freddy had liked Theo from the very first time he'd come by for an interview. Freddy knew he had to be cool since he was a Cardboard Camp instructor. But then he'd learned Theo knew how to shoot an actual longbow (the kind they use in the *Lord of the Rings* movies!), *and* he earned extra money on weekends by drawing those crazy caricature portraits at random art and music festivals in his spare time.

"Right?" Theo agreed, taking a swig of his milk. "There's the theme of your room, Fred. Solved. Bees and Breakfast."

Freddy inhaled sharply, then blurted out a laugh. He leaned over to high-five their B&B host, but Lucy reached out and blocked it. "No," she said. "We cannot build a plexiglass wall to *show* the bees at work. We're under a tight deadline here, and that's a nice-to-have, not a need-to-have."

Freddy glared back at her.

"Lucy's right," Dad agreed.

Lila shrugged. "To be honest, the cost of removing that whole wall and replacing it with plexiglass—not to mention the job of keeping the bees safe and *not* attacking while we did that kind of work—would cost a whole lot more than just moving them. Sorry, Freddy."

With Theo's suggestion officially vetoed, they all returned their attention to the matter of bee *removal*. Freddy and Kassy explained the process to everyone, and then dropped the price. "It's gonna be a few thousand bucks," Freddy said, watching Dad's face as he said it.

"I'm done," Dad said, closing his eyes and slumping back in his chair. "That just stings."

Freddy and Theo both laughed but quieted quickly when they realized Dad's pun—*stings . . . bees*—hadn't been intentional.

"I'd be willing to give up the rest of my share of the winnings from the Ohio Food Truck Festival to help pay for it," Lucy said quickly.

"Same," Herb offered.

Freddy paused. They had split the Food Truck Festival

winnings in equal fourths, which left each of the Peaches with $2,500. They'd each already chipped in $1,000 of their winnings to furnish the B&B guest rooms. Freddy had been excited to spend the rest of his share on something like real metal armor for next year's Cardboard Camp, or maybe a 3D printer. "I'm in, too," Freddy said. If it came down to him buying some unnecessary new stuff, or helping fix his family and their home, the choice was simple. "Between the three of us, we can cover the cost, Dad."

Dad opened his eyes just a sliver. "Okay."

"Okay?" Freddy confirmed.

Dad nodded. Before he could say anything more, Lila cut in. "Kassy and I can call the bee people tomorrow and figure out how soon they can get here to sort stuff out. And we'll patch up whatever mess they make of the wall afterward. No charge. We helped cause the problem."

"Thank you," Dad said softly. After a long pause, Dad admitted, "My cousin David keeps calling, nudging me to get on board with the idea of selling this place. Well, it's actually more of a push than a nudge—and I know he's working the same angle with Great Aunt Lucinda. Every time another problem comes up, it's really tempting to listen to him."

"I don't want to just let this house go," Lucy moaned. "We need to fight back." Freddy knew that his sister, possibly more than any of them, loved the rickety old mansion. But Lucy also hated *failure* more than any of them, so he had a feeling that she also really didn't want to flop in their quest to convert the Peach Pit into a perfect B&B.

"None of us want to let it go," Herb agreed. Freddy noticed that the dogs were all sitting in a perfect line beside Herb's chair, waiting patiently for the balls of sausage Herb was slipping them quietly under the table.

"I finished designing a guest book this week," Lucy said quickly. "And we have Theo on the team now to help with a lot of the little stuff we need to figure out before David and Great Aunt Lucinda check in for opening weekend. We have a ton of breakfast recipes ready to go."

Dad grabbed a slice of pizza, but his hand stilled halfway to his mouth. "We have a little of Mom's fun money left over, but not much. We'll just have to make do with that, and if we run out before everything's ready, well . . ." Dad stopped. The thing was, Freddy knew there wasn't anywhere they could turn for help. They couldn't ask Great Aunt Lucinda for money, since she had already given them a whole *house.* She was giving up a lot of her own personal money by offering to hand them a house, no charge, when she needed the money for her own retirement. And Dad's cousin David wasn't about to offer them cash to help with something he thought was a "crazy plan." So they were going to have to make this work—to *finish*—with what remaining money and energy they had. If they couldn't do it, they'd need to move on and let someone else grow the Peach Pit into something wonderful.

"You think I want to sell this house to the highest bidder?" Dad blurted out suddenly, his cheeks growing pink. "No. I want to keep it in the family just as much as any of you. This house is stuffed with history. And inside that history is our story—mine, and yours, and *ours*—and it's exactly where I want to build some of our family's future memories."

Freddy blinked. He wasn't used to his dad being so expressive. Clearly, the Peach Pit had grown on all of them. But that was because *they'd* been the ones nurturing it, in order to help it grow.

Dad set his mouth in a firm line. He glanced at each of his kids. "We deserve good things after the past couple years. So I'm going to fight as hard as I can to keep us here. Just like all of you are doing."

As they cleaned up after dinner, Freddy considered what Dad had said: That the Peach Pit was stuffed with history, and inside that history was a story. *Their* story.

There was a ton of history crammed into the old house, and bits and pieces of their family's story were hidden inside each wall and broken doorknob and old toilet they'd pulled out of the house over these past weeks. Suddenly, Freddy realized exactly what he needed to do to build his art project with the personal touch he'd been searching for all this time. He could use cast-off pieces of the Peach Pit to build his treehouse art installation! By doing this, he would create his own style of art *and* preserve important pieces of their family history in one gorgeous sculpture.

A family tree of sorts. "The Peach Family Treehouse!" he blurted out just as Dad pulled the full garbage bag out of the can under the sink. "I'll take out the trash," Freddy offered. He tossed on a pair of shoes and ran outside. He threw the garbage bag in the plastic bin at the end of the driveway, then raced over to the dumpster that was stuffed full of old construction debris and pipes and plaster and wood chunks that had been dragged out of the house. Now that he knew what he wanted to do, Freddy was eager to begin his hunt for the perfect building materials. He finally had the right plan, and he couldn't wait to start.

It was freezing cold outside, but Freddy had a thick sweatshirt on, so even the soft dusting of snow that covered the edges of the dumpster (and everything inside it) was hardly noticeable.

Freddy hopped up onto the edge of the dumpster and lowered himself down into a century's worth of Peach family history. Almost as soon as he was inside the pile of rubble, he saw it. A perfect base from which to grow his sculpture: the old toilet they'd pulled out of Freddy's very own guest suite! "A latrine is the heart of a house and the one thing that all members of a family have in common," Freddy said aloud in a royal accent, beating his chest with one fist as he chuckled to himself. "Just think of all the family history *this* throne has witnessed."

From the Sketchbook of Freddy Peach:

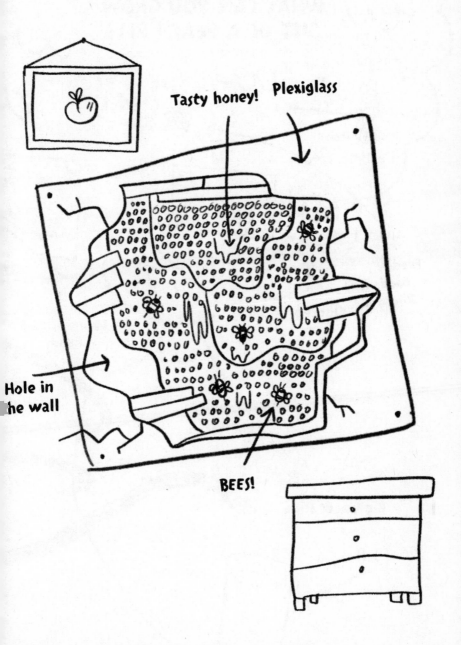

Tasty honey!

Plexiglass

Hole in the wall

BEES!

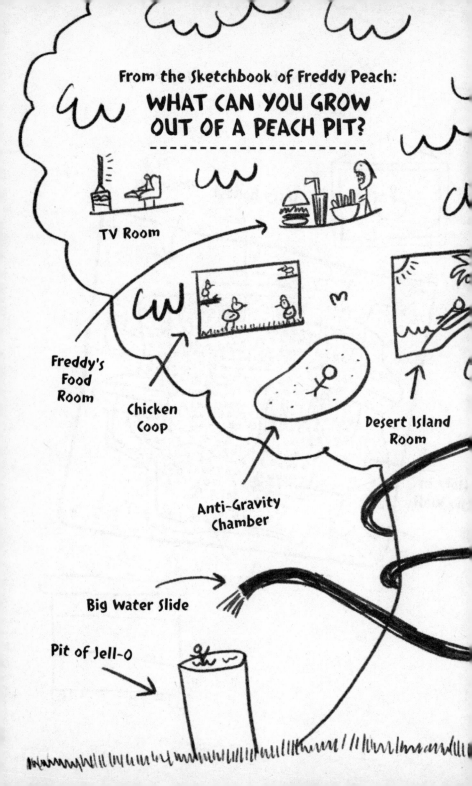

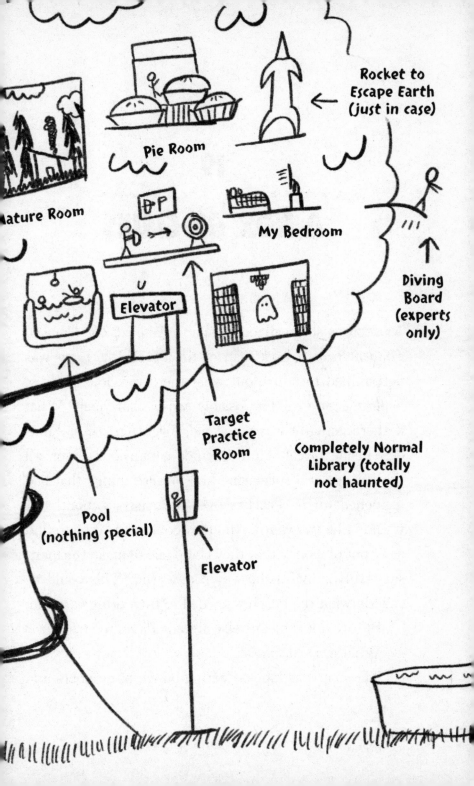

Rocket to Escape Earth (just in case)

Pie Room

Nature Room

My Bedroom

Diving Board (experts only)

Elevator

Target Practice Room

Completely Normal Library (totally not haunted)

Pool (nothing special)

Elevator

19

A BOX OF CLUES

As soon as she realized the paper labeled *The Hunt for Hidden Riches* was a map of the Peach Pit, Lucy was determined to figure out what the mysterious piece of paper meant. Could it possibly *be* a treasure map? What if there actually was some old, forgotten *treasure* hidden inside Great Aunt Lucinda's mansion? After all the strange and surprising and bizarre things that had happened to the Peaches over the past six months, it wouldn't be *that* weird. And how cool would it be to find a big pot of money that they could use to make the mansion truly shine in the way it deserved? This could be exactly what the Peaches needed to turn things around.

But what if someone else already found the treasure? What if *no one* had?

The map was labeled with a bunch of numbers and

lines that didn't seem to make any sense. The number one was drawn in her bedroom on the map; was she just supposed to start digging around for random stuff or clues that might be hidden? With twelve numbers in total, this hunt could take her a lifetime.

After poring over the map with Maren—who had offered to scan the map using her mom's fancy scanner and then upload it to a computer to adjust the resolution so the lines were darker and clearer—Lucy began to wonder if she was missing some key piece. Had she overlooked something? Another clue of some kind that she needed to help her solve the hunt?

She'd already scoured the entire attic and hadn't found anything else that looked useful. But she figured two sets of eyes were better than one, so she invited her best friend over that weekend to help her expand the search. They decided to start in the spot where Lucy had first found the map.

"Do *not* tell my brothers this trapdoor exists," Lucy told Maren as she led her to the secret door in the ceiling of her closet. "So far, neither of them has noticed me sneaking up here, and I want to keep it that way."

"Understood," Maren said, easily hoisting herself up into the attic space. "Whoa . . . this is amazing, Luce."

Lucy grinned. "Isn't it?"

Over the past couple months, Lucy had been spending whatever free time she could spare digging through and tidying up the attic mess. She'd organized the boxes, stacked crates and bins, and washed the windows. She'd swept the floor and pulled a couple of old pieces of lawn furniture into a back corner near one of the windows to create a sort of reading nook. She'd covered the grimy wicker furniture with spare blankets that had been tucked away in closets in some of the guest rooms, and found a cute woven rug that she laid down on the floor to make it feel even more homey.

"You should move up here," Maren said, peeking into some of the boxes before flopping down on one of the chairs.

"It's not insulated," Lucy pointed out. This was one of the things she'd learned a lot about over the past few months, by shadowing—and listening to—the Handy Gals. Insulation was super important in an old house like this, to help keep heating costs down in the winter, and to help keep the house cool in the summer. Dad had explained that it would cost a fortune to heat a house this size through a Duluth winter, but luckily Great Aunt Lucinda had updated and improved the wall insulation in much of the house over the years. This—and semi-regularly getting the outside of the house painted—was one of the few things she had done to help keep the house from crumbling into a total money pit. There were a lot of problems Aunt Lucinda had ignored, but she hadn't ignored *everything*. "I'd freeze to death in the winter, and I bet it gets to be at least a hundred degrees up here when it's super hot in the summer."

"Oh," Maren said, shrugging. "Okay, so maybe don't move up here permanently, but we should totally have a sleepover up here sometime."

"That would be super fun," Lucy agreed. Then she remembered the idea she'd been considering that would be even *more* fun. "Hey, do you maybe want to spend the night this weekend and be a practice guest at the B and B? You can stay in my room—The Winter Suite—and let me know if it's comfortable, or if you notice anything missing for you to have a good night's sleep and a comfortable stay?"

Maren laughed. "You sound like the front desk lady at the hotel my swim team stays at for our state swim meet."

"That's good!" Lucy said, laughing along with her. "Because sometimes I will be the front desk lady at a hotel, starting in just a couple weeks."

Maren shook her head. "That's so weird. What's with your dad and all these random jobs he keeps making you guys do—first baking pies and selling them out of a food truck all summer? Now, being construction people and working in your own house that's also kind of a hotel?"

"It's not *that* weird," Lucy said, bristling a bit. She knew it was hard for her friends to understand her family and their strange quirks, but the thing was, in some bizarre way, running a B&B totally fit their family. It would have been a *better* fit if their mom were still alive, since she was the one who most loved meeting new people and loved taking the seed of an idea and growing it into something exciting and new. But Lucy and Freddy and Herb had all inherited important pieces of their mom that made them a perfect combo to take on a challenge like this in her absence. "Okay, so maybe not *all* families would want to run a food truck or a bed-and-breakfast, but our family seems to do really well with these kinds of challenges. It's something interesting for us to do together and honestly, Mar? It's fun. And I'm learning a lot."

"Yeah," Maren said. "My family would probably kill each other if we had to camp out together all summer or live through this construction mess. But I guess your family is one of those special types that can handle it."

Yeah, Lucy thought to herself. *The Peaches are special.*

The way her family's lives had shaken out over the past few years wasn't normal or boring or easy by most people's standards. But what *was* normal when it came to families? Every family was built differently, and each type of family needed to figure out how they worked best. The Peaches had proven that they were capable of surviving—even thriving—through chaos and challenges. Like a piece of build-it-yourself furniture, theirs was a special collection of lots of different kinds of parts (made up of Lucy-Freddy-Herb-Dad) that had begun to click and lock into the exact right spot. "So, do you want to help me figure out how to follow this treasure map to hidden riches, or what?" Lucy said, shifting back to the main reason she and Maren had come up to the attic.

"Absolutely," Maren said. She pulled a folded piece of paper out of her pocket and held it up. "This is the scan of the original map, with the contrast set really high. So the lines are as dark as we can get them now. It's still not super clear, but on this copy the numbers are easier to read than they were on the original."

Lucy and Maren sat together on the rug on the floor of the attic and pored over the treasure map. Now that the lines were darker, thanks to Maren's mom's scanner and some clever fiddling with the file, Lucy was a little embarrassed she hadn't immediately realized it was a map of the Peach Pit. It was so *obviously* a map of this house—but what did the map and the random little boxes and numbers mean?

"I can't figure out if the map is *telling* me something about where to look for the hidden riches, or if it's just a map and I'm missing something that would explain what all the lines and numbers mean?" She pointed. "I wish there was just an *X* that told me where to dig."

"If there was an *X* to mark the spot, that wouldn't make this hunt for hidden riches very fun," Maren pointed out. She wiggled her eyebrows. "What if the map leads you to some kind of *actual* treasure? I mean, what if there's a chest full of jewels, or cash, or stolen vases and paintings or something?"

"Let's hope we don't find stolen vases and paintings," Lucy said, cringing. "That would make the Peach Pit the scene of a crime, and Great Aunt Lucinda a criminal, and *that's* not going to help convince her son that we should keep the house in the family." She sighed. "I hope whatever we find at the end of this treasure map is worth *something*, at least. If we find some sort of treasure, Dad's cousin David might get off our case. We could hand over something of value, and then he wouldn't have to sell the house. And we'd definitely get to stay here. Everyone wins."

"Yeah, that makes sense." Maren handed Lucy the map and closed her eyes. "Do you think we just need to follow the map from the first number to the last and see what we find?"

"Maybe?" Lucy shrugged. "But we don't have any idea what we're looking for along the way. Are there clues, or arrows, or some other reason that we're supposed to follow the numbers?"

Maren flopped onto her back and stared up at the attic eaves. "Is there a safe anywhere in the house?" she asked. "Maybe the numbers are a code for a safe that's hidden in room number twelve?"

"No safe," Lucy said. "I've explored every corner of this house, and unless it's super well-hidden, there's no safe. I've looked extra carefully in the attic, and also in the living room, since that's where the number twelve seems to be on the map."

"Isn't the *point* of a safe to be super well-hidden?" Maren asked, lifting her eyebrows. "Don't people usually hide them in the wall behind old paintings or bookshelves or something? This house was *made* for a safe. Think about all the art that's hanging on the walls."

"I mean . . ." Lucy said, cocking her head. "I guess it's possible. Wanna look some more?"

For the next hour, she and Maren scoured every inch of the house. They went in the order the numbers on the map told them to. All the guest bedrooms were immediately deemed unlikely, since they'd all been pulled apart and put back together and no one had found any hidden safes during that process. They snuck into Dad's,

Freddy's, and Herb's bedrooms and peeked behind all the shelves and in the closets, and moved aside Great Aunt Lucinda's ugly painting of a giant bowl of pears that Dad had kept hanging in his room. Lucy felt a little bad about snooping, but if it led them to hidden riches that would help convince Dad's cousin David to let them keep the Peach Pit, it was worth the invasion of privacy.

They looked in the kitchen, inside the servant staircases, opened every closet door, and even pushed and tapped at the walls in the bathrooms. When they finally gave up their hunt and stopped in the kitchen for one of Freddy's fresh-baked cookies, the girls spread the map out in front of them and studied it again.

"We have a bunch of numbers on a piece of paper we're pretty sure is a house map, and nothing else to go on," Maren said softly, making sure neither of the boys overheard her. They were both in their bedrooms, but Lucy didn't want to risk them listening in.

Lucy sighed. "We have a garage out back, and there's a ton of stuff crammed in there. It's gross, but maybe there's something hiding a clue? According to Herb, the garage probably used to be an old horse stall, back in the early twentieth century. Now it's a leaky building that we can't park in because the door is blocked off by the dumpster."

Maren grinned. "It's worth looking."

Together, they raced to the garage. Inside, Lucy scanned the shelves for something, anything. Most of the contents in the garage were tools and garden supplies, but on the topmost shelf in the farthest corner were a bunch of board games. And on the very bottom of the stack, there was a very old, very dusty Monopoly box. "Mar!" Lucy called out. "Monopoly is all about making money, right? And this is the Hunt for Hidden Riches, so . . ."

Maren shrieked when she saw Lucy reach for it and pull it off the shelf. The box was almost falling apart, but inside, the game and all the pieces and the piles of paper money were still intact. Lucy felt a bubble of excitement in her stomach. Maybe they were on the right track . . .

"Do you see a note or anything?" Maren asked as Lucy pawed through the game pieces and all the paper money. "Is there any real cash inside the box?"

She and Maren pulled the whole game apart, digging and searching through everything in the box, eager to find a clue or a prize or a note or *something*.

"Nothing," Lucy said finally, tossing a whole fistful of Monopoly money into the air, watching as it floated to the ground around her. "This is a dead end."

"Ugh!" Maren groaned. "We're no closer to finding

hidden riches than we were three hours ago. What now?"

"Now I keep searching," Lucy said with a shrug. "Peaches don't quit."

GUEST REGISTRY
Have a PEACHY Stay!

Name	Date of Arrival	Date of Departure
Name	Date of Arrival	Date of Departure
Name	Date of Arrival	Date of Departure
Name	Date of Arrival	Date of Departure
Name	Date of Arrival	Date of Departure
Name	Date of Arrival	Date of Departure

Breakfast will be from 7AM to 11AM every day!
Report to the front desk with questions.

FREDDY'S PEACH PIT "WELCOME" COOKIES

1. Beat together until super pale (like 2–3 minutes):
   - **2 sticks of butter**
   - **1 C brown sugar**
   - **1/2 C white sugar**
2. Then mix in:
   - **2 eggs**
   - **1 t vanilla (or more if you want)**
3. When that's all yummy looking and smooth, add:
   - **2 1/4–2 1/2 C flour**
   - **1 t salt**
   - **1 t baking soda**
   - **1 C oats**
   - **1 bag of chocolate chips/chocolate chunks or M&Ms**

   If you use an electric mixer, be careful not to turn it on too fast or your flour will fly everywhere!

4. Once the batter is ready, stir in (by hand) 1 bag of chocolate chips/chocolate chunks or M&Ms!
5. Bake them at 375° F for about 6–10 minutes, depending on how big your cookie balls are.

VARIATIONS:

*   Swap chocolate hazelnut spread or peanut butter for some of the butter.
*   Add broken-up pretzel pieces for extra crunch!
*   Toss in some nuts (not my fave).
*   Sprinkle salt on the top of each cookie right after they come out of the oven!
*   Use butterscotch chips instead of chocolate chips.

20

DOGS' DAY OUT

The weekend before Thanksgiving, with less than a week to go before their grand opening, all four Peaches and a pair of dogs (Vix and Dasher—the only two willing to wear a collar and leash) made a trek to the Birch Pond retirement community to visit Great Aunt Lucinda and her friends. Though they had a million things to do back at the Peach Pit, they'd agreed to spend the evening playing Hearts with Aunt Lucinda—a continuation of their years'-long tournament of the Two Lucindas versus the Peach Boys. But first, they would all get to enjoy Birch Pond's Fall Feast, a special Saturday when each of the residents got to nominate snacks and desserts for the center's cooks to whip up, and everyone who lived at the center was allowed to invite family to come for an afternoon social. Herb was excited to give his family the grand tour of his place of business and introduce them to some of the people he'd begun to think of as family. But he was even *more* excited to debut Vix and Dasher's improved behavior and tricks for Great Aunt Lucinda and her friends.

When they pulled into the Birch Pond parking lot, Herb fastened a leash to each dog's collar and told them both to sit. Vix awkwardly sat on Freddy's lap, and Dash half-sat half-hovered on the bump in the center of the back seat. "Now, I want you both on your best behavior," Herb told them, using his most commanding voice. "No peeing on shoes, no chewing, and *no* monkey business."

"Think they understand you?" Freddy asked, looking very much like he thought not. "Did you know that most dogs understand somewhere between one hundred and two hundred words, which is about the same as a human two- or three-year-old?" He laughed. "But I'd argue that these guys are definitely not as smart as your average human toddler."

Herb shushed him. "That's not helping. We need to boost their confidence before their big visit, not hurt their feelings."

Dad popped open the trunk and grabbed the box full of fresh-baked pies he'd brought to serve during the Fall Feast. "I miss doing something as simple as baking pies," Dad had explained when he'd called Great Aunt Lucinda to tell her he was bringing dessert to share. "This B and B project is so big and feels never-ending, so the simple act of baking a pie is actually really satisfying. There's a clear beginning, middle, and end. The Peach Pit renovation feels like one long middle, and it's deeply unsettling." Dad had been a ball of nerves the past few weeks, especially with his cousin David breathing down their necks. He'd burned the first two pies, but his later efforts all turned out pretty well.

Herb knew his dad liked to follow a process when he did things. Herb did, too; it's one of the reasons he enjoyed math so much. There was a natural path to follow that eventually led to a clear solution. But unlike math, the mansion renovation was definitely not following a clear path. There were endless random tasks, each of which led to more projects and problems, and whenever it seemed like they were close to solving something, a new variable popped into the equation that messed everything up.

The chaos and constant craziness were making everyone in the Peach family a little nutso, for different reasons. Even though his bedroom was never tidy and didn't always *look* clean, Herb actually loved order and organization. This was one of the reasons he'd been enjoying setting up both the dollhouse and his new secret cellar space so much. Ever since the day when he'd discovered the magical space hiding under the Peach Pit, Herb had taken the time to sweep a lot of the dirt and cobwebs and dead bugs to the farthest corners, in order to begin the slow process of moving his collections out of his bedroom and into their new spots in his hidden treasure chest.

He had a shelf for pine cones and other magnificent things he'd found in nature.

There was a shelf for lost-and-now-found stuffies and old, mismatched socks.

One whole wall was filled with the various "tips" he'd received for his work at Birch Pond—hundreds of buttons, nearly a dozen Beanie Babies, a glass jar with a collection of hard candy Herb didn't particularly like, and a wide variety of activity books and toys and trinkets that had obviously meant something to someone once (and now meant a whole lot to Herb!).

He'd also created a space dedicated to memories of his mom. Here he lined up some of her old shampoo bottles; a few favorite pictures he'd slid out of family albums; Post-it notes with her handwriting that he'd found in a desk drawer after she'd died that no one ever cleaned out; and the old plastic food truck he and his mom used to play with together when Herb was little. Herb had turned it into a Peach Pie Truck, to help him remember their family's fun adventure the previous summer.

Over the past week, Herb had begun to convert part of the cellar floor and some of the bottom shelves into a fun playland for some of the house mice. He'd set up tunnels and ramps made out of toilet paper tubes and cardboard—just like he'd done for his mouse babies that summer on their family road trip—and set out tasty snacks like peanut butter and cheese so the little critters who lived down there would know Herb was a friend. He didn't want them to think he was trying to steal their space and kick them out!

Even Dasher had begun to get used to the little mice bustling around them in the cellar. In fact, as they headed from the car to the Birch Pond front entrance that chilly

Saturday morning for the Fall Feast, Dash was only mildly distracted by all the small squirrels skittering to and fro on the center's lawn; Vix, on the other hand, went absolutely nuts for them. She strained at her leash and harness, desperately trying to chase every squirrel she saw off the property. Herb was tugged this way and that, and soon he was entirely tangled up in the two leashes. As Vix scampered and barked, she wrapped her leash around and through Herb's legs until Herb went toppling to the frost-covered ground.

"*Oof!*" Herb moaned as he hit the frozen grass. Unwilling to let go of the leashes, lest Vix or Dash took off across the center's sprawling lawn, Herb was quickly tangled up in something that resembled a spider's web made out of lengths of leash. "A little help here?" he squeaked.

Lucy raced over to untangle her brother, but as soon as Vix had some slack on her leash, she lunged for a squirrel racing up a tree trunk, taking Lucy down in the process. As she hit the ground, she dropped the leash and Vix made a run for it.

Freddy dove, grabbing the pup's harness before Vix could make it very far. Flustered, Dad set down his box of pies to try to help control the chaos. But as soon as he stepped away from his baked goods,

Dasher—who'd probably been waiting quietly for this exact opportunity—perched his front paws on the rim of the box and greedily nosed into an apple pie.

By the time the Peaches got inside Birch Pond's lobby, they were all cold, a little muddy, and covered in mushed-up apple pie. "The dogs' big day out is going really well so far," Freddy said cheerfully.

Herb glared at him. This was not how it was supposed to go! He'd had such big plans, and nothing was going the way it should. *It's okay*, Herb told himself. Now that they were inside, in a squirrel-free zone, the dogs would surely be better behaved. They had been working so hard at their training, and he just knew they could handle their big Birch Pond debut.

"My babies!" Great Aunt Lucinda came hustling through the lobby, bending down to greet the two dogs with kisses and ear scratches. "Oh, how I've missed my little darlings!"

Aunt Lucinda let the dogs jump and squirm all over her. She was wearing a huge smile and an even huger Dolly Parton wig atop her head. Herb had seen her wear this long, poufy blond wig a few times before, but it was always fun to see her in it. He wondered if the wig was heavy, and if her neck got sore holding so much hair on top of her head. Some wigs, he'd learned from Freddy, were made with real hair and some were fake hair—the big difference between the two kinds was price.

"How much did that wig cost?" Freddy blurted out as Great Aunt Lucinda wrapped him into a side-arm hug.

"Wig?" Great Aunt Lucinda said with a wink. "What wig? This is my own natural God-given hair, Fred."

Freddy laughed. "Did you know the artist Andy Warhol's wig sold for more than ten thousand dollars? It was made out of real hair, and I guess it was pretty famous."

"What a stupid way to spend that much money," Lucy announced. "Think of how far ten thousand bucks would go in the Peach Pit!"

"Not far," Walter Peach muttered.

Herb groaned, trying to calm the dogs back down again.

Aunt Lucinda laughed. "Do I even want to ask how things are going?" she asked. "It's almost time for the big reveal." She wiggled her fingers in the air like confetti.

"The renovation is—" Walter Peach began.

"—coming along great!" Freddy interrupted. "Lucy's room is almost ready to welcome you as our first official guest, and the other two guest rooms will be all set by the time David arrives."

Herb stared at his brother. Was he bonkers? Things were definitely *not* great. There was no way the B&B would be ready by the time their first VIP guests arrived. They had so much left to do, and hardly any time to do it.

"There is nothing for you to worry about," Lucy added.

That's when Herb realized his family was telling a little fib on *purpose*. They were trying to make Aunt Lucinda feel better, since having *her* worry wasn't going to make things go any better for them. This was what Herb would call a friendly fib. One of those *little* lies that didn't really hurt anyone, but telling it maybe still wasn't the best idea.

"Well, I'm counting on you to not let me down. Don't give David the opportunity to doubt me and my decisions. We're all in this together." Great Aunt Lucinda winked again, and Herb's tummy rolled with nerves. She bent down to let the pups lick her face. Vix and Dasher leaped and spun and nibbled at Great Aunt Lucinda's wig. "You smell so good, my babies," Aunt Lucinda cooed. "Like fresh apples and butter!"

Dad cleared his throat and said, "We brought pie."

"How thoughtful," Great Aunt Lucinda said, standing up to give him a kiss on each cheek. She also hugged

Herb, even though they'd just seen each other the previous afternoon. "Now come on through to the lounge; that's where they're setting up the Fall Feast. Herb, honey, you can put the pups in my apartment during the party so you don't have to worry about them eating any more of the food."

While his family followed Great Aunt Lucinda to the lounge, Herb headed down the hallway toward her apartment. He'd put the dogs in her bedroom so they could rest and stay out of trouble during the feast. But before settling them down for their nap, Herb decided to stop in to visit a few of his friends so they could meet Vix and Dash. At each stop, the two dogs behaved marvelously, acting perfect as people offered them scraps of bacon and cubes of cheese in exchange for a successful *Sit* or *Lay Down* or *Stay*. Diane and Caroline were hanging out together in Caroline's apartment, and Herb proudly showed the two of them how nicely both dogs could *Shake* (the newest trick Herb had been working on with the pack).

Before heading into Great Aunt Lucinda's apartment, Herb took the two pups outside for a quick pee. Just as he was coming back in, Herb bumped into grumpy Joye, who was headed toward the lobby. Herb waved at her and tightened the dogs' leashes, fully prepared for Joye to scowl back and tell him to keep his distance. But in a complete twist, Joye smiled and clapped to get the dogs' attention. She made kissing noises at them, patting her leg to try to get the dogs to come over to meet her. They pawed at her leg, and Joye absolutely lit up. Herb gaped at her. She was laughing as she petted and cuddled them. This could not be the Joye he knew. Did Joye have a secret (friendly) twin he hadn't yet met?!

"Who is this?" Joye blurted, pointing at Vix.

"That's Vixen," Herb told her. "And this one is Dasher."

"Where are the other two dogs?" Joye snapped, frowning at him.

"They had to stay home," Herb explained. "They're not ready for public outings just yet."

Joye glared at him. "Give me the leashes."

Startled, Herb did as he was told.

"You can head on in to the Fall Feast now," Joye ordered. "I've got these two under control. I'm not much for parties, so they should spend the afternoon at my place where they won't have to be alone." Without waiting for Herb to answer, she and the dogs wandered off down the hall, leaving Herb to stare and wonder what had just happened.

"Joye!" Herb called out. Joye glanced over her shoulder with a frown. "Can I come, too?"

"Suit yourself," Joye said. So Herb traipsed along

behind her and Vix and Dash, eager to see what Joye's apartment looked like. Since she had never asked Herb to come in and help her with any chores, Herb had never been inside her place. He'd only imagined what it might be like—he'd assumed it would be full of hardwood furniture and beige walls with nothing fun or friendly. But his assumptions were all wrong.

Joye's apartment was painted a cheerful yellow—a complete contrast to her grumpy personality—and the walls were full of homemade art and photos of kids and teenagers and adults doing all sorts of fun things: swimming in lakes, waterskiing, posing in Halloween costumes, throwing cake in one another's faces, dancing around a bonfire. There were even a few pictures of Joye, one with her riding in a hot air balloon and another big framed photo that showed her squeezed onto a small couch along with a whole bunch of babies and kids who were crawling all over her. "Who's this?" Herb asked, pointing to a boy who looked about his age in the couch photo.

"That's my grandson, Jake," Joye said, settling into a recliner in one corner of the small living room. When she patted her leg, Dash and Vix both climbed up onto her lap. Joye rubbed their ears and sighed happily. "He's about your age."

"Does he ever come to visit you?" Herb asked.

"They come once a year, around Christmas," Joye said. "That's when we took that picture last year."

"He lives far away?" Herb guessed.

"Jake and his family are out in Vermont," Joye said.

"Do you miss them?" Herb wandered around the room, looking at all the pictures of smiling family. He found more shots of Joye, looking happy and so very friendly.

"Of course I miss them," Joye snapped. Then her face softened and she added, "I wish I could travel to see them more, but it's hard to get so far away. I don't have much choice but to wait here for them to come to me. I miss them all the time, but that's the way it is."

Herb nodded. He sat primly on the very edge of Joye's sofa, surprised to discover it was squishy and inviting. He settled in deeper, letting the couch hug him in close. Suddenly, Herb very much missed his mom. She'd also been so snuggly. Mom had always been the one to wrap him in a towel after his baths, and then she'd pull him onto her lap and cuddle him close. Dad was great, too, but he wasn't squishy the way Mom had been. "I understand," Herb said. "I miss my mom, too, but I never get to see her anymore."

"That can't be easy," Joye said, nodding. "You don't even get once a year at Christmas."

Herb shook his head. "And then there's dumb stuff that's always reminding me that she's gone—like the stinky Mother-Son Tea at school."

"I thought you were going to talk to your teacher about that," Joye said, rubbing Vix's ears between her thumb and finger. Herb was surprised she remembered them talking about it. He'd always assumed Joye was just waiting for him to leave so she could be alone with her friends. But maybe, he was suddenly realizing, she just got grouchy when Herb was around because it reminded her that her grandkids couldn't come for a visit as often as he visited Great Aunt Lucinda.

"I don't want Mr. Andrus to get mad at me," Herb explained.

"Your teacher won't get mad at you for telling him that," Joye grumbled. "He needs to know it's causing a problem. Might be that you're not the only one having a hard time with this event. Maybe by speaking up you'll be helping more kids than just yourself."

"I don't even know how to bring it up," Herb said, settling deeper into the soft couch. He pulled his legs under himself, curling up like a cat. "I'm afraid I'll lose all my words and just stand there and forget what I was going to say."

"Get your dirty socks off my sofa," Joye snapped.

Then, in a softer voice, she said, "Why don't you write your teacher a letter? That way you can say everything you want to say, and you won't forget because you're feeling nervous."

A letter. Herb hadn't thought about that. He could have Lucy help him write it, and that way, Mr. Andrus could read it on his own time, when Herb wasn't standing right there in front of him. "Okay," Herb said. "A letter. I'll write him a letter. Thanks, Joye."

Joye nodded. "Now, get out of here and get yourself over to the Fall Feast. Leave me in peace to nap with the dogs."

Dear Mr. Andrus,

I really like having you as my teacher. You are very nice and funny and I think your morning book club is cool and I like that you have so many good books to read in your classroom. But I am sad about something and I think I should tell you. The Mother-Son Tea isn't fair to kids like me. I don't have a mom anymore because she died when I was in kindergarten. There are maybe other kids who don't have a mom because they have two dads, or live with their grandparents or an uncle or a foster family or some other adult that is not a mom.

Being invited to things like a Mother-Son Tea doesn't help me feel better about not having my mom. I wish you would rename it so that it would be fair to everyone. Maybe you could call it the Special Person Tea. That's just one idea.

From,
Herb Peach
Third Grade Student at Lakeside
Elementary School

PS: If you change the name and I can come to the tea (because I don't need to have a mom to get to go), I can bring some pies to share with everyone. My dad makes the best pies.

PS #2: Dad is not the person I would invite as my special person to your tea party. He's great, but he does not like tea and there is someone else who I think would really like to come with me, even though I think she would pretend it is awful.

21

WHAT CAN YOU GROW OUT OF A PEACH PIT?

The weekend visit to Birch Pond ended in the best possible way—according to Freddy, anyway. After the Fall Feast had wrapped up, and they'd played more than a dozen games of Hearts, Dad declared that it was past his bedtime and they ought to be getting home.

"For the record, it's six-fifteen," Freddy announced. "Your bedtime is usually ten-twenty-six, right after the local weather forecast on the news."

"It's been a big day," Dad replied tersely. "And we have to get a good night's sleep, since we have a lot of work to do on the house tomorrow and the rest of this week if we're going to have things ready to go for Lucinda and David's visit next weekend."

Next weekend. Freddy gulped. They had less than four days to finish up the B&B for Opening Day, or else they would be preparing for Moving Day. The construction pieces of Freddy's guest room project had finally wrapped up, but he was nowhere close to having it ready to go for guests. Luckily, Lucy's room looked great. And Dad and Herb were making good progress on The Fruit Suite. But Freddy was having a really hard time getting everything done. Between his art show project, and his schoolwork, and everything they needed to finish at the B&B—there just wasn't enough time!

Freddy worked well under pressure, so there was still hope. But he had so much to do, and he had definitely come to realize there might not be enough hours in the day.

While Lucy packed up the playing cards and quietly talked with Great Aunt Lucinda, Herb got the dogs ready to go and Freddy munched on the remnants of pie. When they were all ready, Herb let the dogs lead the way out into the hall. A game of Bingo was just about to start in the lounge, so the hallways at Birch Pond were full of people and activity.

Herb stopped to greet every single person they passed, and a bunch of random old people petted the dogs and asked Freddy and Lucy questions. Around so many people, Freddy instantly switched into businessman mode and began inviting people to come and have a weekend away at the Peachy Keen B&B (this was the name he'd been chewing on that week). He promised to stop by Birch Pond to deliver business cards "soon," and talked up their world-famous apple muffins and "Welcome Cookies."

"What are you *doing*?" Lucy hissed during a lull in conversation.

"Advertising our digs!" Freddy said, waving to a man with a walker who was wandering down the hall in a bathrobe and Adidas slides.

"We don't *have* 'digs,'" Lucy said, glaring at him. "We barely have a single room ready for Great Aunt Lucinda to stay in later this week. Unless we get a move on, David is going to be sleeping on the couch. Stop telling people to 'plan their next getaway at the Peachy Keen B and B'!" Lucy growled. "That name is awful, by the way. We really need to pick a real one. Like, yesterday."

Just then, Freddy noticed that Herb had let go of both dogs' leashes so they could run down the hall to greet two women. One of the women—Diane, Freddy was pretty sure her name was—knelt down to swoop up Vixen as she raced toward her. But Vix did a swerve and maneuvered around Diane and her friend. Dash, meanwhile, *dashed* past both of the women on the other side of the hall. Freddy stood on tiptoe to try to see where the pups were headed. At the far end of the hall, the man in a bathrobe had stopped in front of an open door. The two pups squirmed past the guy's walker and raced inside the room. But as they scooted past him, Vix grabbed the tie of the man's robe and tugged. The tie came undone and the fluffy bathrobe slid off, leaving the man standing in the middle of the hall in a bright yellow-and-orange-flowered swimsuit.

"Oh no!" Herb screeched. "I'm sorry, Kurt!"

The man—Kurt, presumably—grinned back at Herb as he stepped through the open door. "I just lost a game of tug-of-war to a ten-pound dog. That's not going to help my stud-factor around here."

All three Peach kids raced down the hall with Herb leading the way. As soon as they reached the open door, Freddy stopped. The glass-paneled door was labeled with the words BIRCH POND THERAPY POOL. The wall next to the door was made of glass, and behind the glass Freddy could see two very wet, very skinny dogs—bobbing and paddling around like they owned the place.

"Dasher! Vix! Here!" Herb cried out desperately. But the dogs paid him no attention.

"Who knew those little rats could swim?" Freddy muttered aloud. He leaned against the wall, watching the action unfold through the glass. Several Birch Pond residents were in the pool, doing some sort of exercise class. The dogs seemed absolutely captivated by an old, cranky-looking woman who was in the class.

"Joye!" Herb called to her. "Can you help me get them out of there? Barb, Maxine, Luis—I'm so sorry they crashed your Water Zumba class!"

Joye, meanwhile, grabbed both dog leashes and pulled Vix and Dasher to the pool stairs, where Herb was waiting. He dragged them out, and the dogs shook themselves—sending a spray of chlorinated water several feet in every direction.

Herb sighed. "Bad dogs," he said wearily. "Sit."

Vix sat, but Dasher tugged and pulled at his leash—ignoring Herb every time he repeated his command.

The grumpy lady called Joye clucked her tongue. "If this is how well it's going with your dog training project, I hate to imagine what that house of Lucinda's is going to look like. . . ."

* * *

When they got home from Birch Pond, Herb and Lucy took the dogs up to the fourth floor to give them a bath after their Water Zumba class. Freddy, meanwhile, waited for his dad to go upstairs to read, and then he snuck out to the shed to work on his art installation.

He'd been putting in a lot of late nights over the past week, and things were finally coming together. But he had to turn in the project for judging on Monday, and there was still a lot to do. Too much. He had until eight o'clock Monday morning to get the piece done, since that's when the Handy Gals were coming by to help him load the project onto their truck bed and deliver it to the community center where the art show was taking place. Freddy wasn't usually prone to panic, but panic was clearly creeping up on him in a less-than-friendly way.

The shed was full of construction leftovers, random thrown-away bits and pieces from the Peach Pit, extra wood he and his friends could eventually use to build the actual treehouse they'd started designing during their school lunch periods, and lots of mostly empty cans of paint, wallpaper, and fabric scraps. After a lot of consideration and sketching and planning and failed starts, Freddy had finally settled into a groove and his project was making perfect sense.

He'd ended up building a mutated, miniature version of his dream treehouse—but he was using only cast-off bits of the Peach Pit to put the whole thing together. The foundation of the house was the old toilet they'd pulled from his guest bedroom, and inside the bowl he'd spread dirt and planted a tiny peach pit to signify the seed from which his project and family had grown. He'd sculpted a tree trunk out of old, rusty plumbing pipes that had been pulled out of the walls and built his whole sculpture around that.

Each of the levels of his treehouse represented something different that he or his family cherished and loved. There was a basketball hoop hanging off the flush handle of the old toilet tank. He'd created a pie room that was built out of scraps and pieces of the old oven that had broken in the kitchen during Lois Sibberson's visit. One story of the treehouse was just a giant pool (a nod to Herb's favorite pastime) that Freddy had created by gluing together shiny, broken pieces of old turquoise tile and shimmering mirrors that had been tossed out of rooms around the house and chucked into the dumpster. For Lucy, there was a library—and he'd constructed tiny little books out of some of Great Aunt Lucinda's beloved fruit art they'd pulled out of rooms around the house. He'd also used a few of Mom's solar clings to fancy up the walls throughout the sculpture. Freddy had drawn and cut out some pictures of their family doing some of the things they'd most enjoyed together before their mom had died. And, of course, there was a miniature food truck crafted out of actual, painted peach pits, perched on the very top of the Peach Pit–scrap sculpture, to represent important pieces of his family's present and future.

He was proud of his work and couldn't wait to share his family's story with the world.

Just as Freddy was dipping a paintbrush in a pot of yellow paint, he heard footsteps in the crackling leaves outside the shed door. "Fred?" Dad's voice called from outside. "Are you in there? Do you know what time it is?"

Freddy didn't wear a watch, so he had no idea what time it was. "Yes. No."

"Son, it's after midnight. What are you doing still up?"

Oops. "What are *you* doing up, Dad?"

Dad opened the door and came inside the shed. He took in the project mess that was scattered all over the space and raked a hand through his wispy hair. Closing the door behind him to keep out the cold, Dad said, "I was catching up on some reading for work and lost track of time."

Freddy gestured around at his own work. "Same."

"The difference is, I'm forty-seven, and you're ten."

"Closer to eleven," Freddy pointed out.

"Doesn't make a difference."

"Well," Freddy argued. "Technically it does."

Dad chuckled. Then he grew serious again. "This is pretty impressive."

"It's not done yet. But it's close."

"Can you tell me about it?" Dad asked.

Freddy walked him through each level of the tree-house, pointing out all of his favorite details and telling him where the building materials for each room had come from. "The piece as a whole is supposed to represent our family, since that's something special that grew out of a Peach Pit."

"It's incredible," Dad said. "How have you found the time to do all this? I can hardly keep up with my work and all the things that need to get done on the house. I hope your schoolwork isn't taking a hit because of all these other projects. School first, right?"

Freddy made a face. In his eyes, school was *never* first. School was a distant *last* that Freddy got to only if and when he had time after all the good stuff was done. Unfortunately, this policy sometimes led to less-than-perfect scores on math tests and reading projects. "I'll have plenty of time to get caught up on school stuff once we open the B and B and I've turned in my art project. Right after Thanksgiving, it's all school, all the time. Promise."

"Fred . . ." Dad warned. "You know the rule. You have to find a balance."

Freddy rolled his eyes.

"You can't let school slide just because there are

other things demanding your attention. It's all about figuring out how to make it all work, and sometimes that means easing up on some things if you can't fit everything in."

Freddy opened his mouth, preparing to argue, but then Dad cut him off.

"I realize I haven't always been a great example of how to find that balance," he said softly. "Take it from me: Juggling all the things you enjoy spending time doing is a lifelong job. It's not always easy to get everything done that I want to get done, but lately I have been getting better at remembering what matters most. And then I make sure I'm devoting plenty of time to that."

"My art matters most," Freddy said. "So shouldn't that come before math?"

Dad sighed. "Much as I admire your passion for business and art and all the big ideas you have swirling around in your head, you do need that good, solid foundation you're going to get in school in order to be successful in either of those fields. As a kid, one of your most important jobs—other than taking care of yourself—is school. I know it's not always your favorite, but it's a non-negotiable and you have to find a way to fit it in with all the other things you're passionate about. So maybe you need to be more selective about how many things you're trying to do at any one time?"

Freddy wasn't entirely sure he *agreed* with this take about *school* being his most important job, but he could understand the basic point of what his dad was saying. "Okay," he said.

"Bed?" Dad asked. But Freddy could tell it was less a question than a command.

"Can we at least negotiate on *that*?" Freddy tried.

"No," Dad said, laughing. "Nice try."

"You really like it?" Freddy asked, gesturing to his sculpture. "Is the toilet foundation too much?"

Dad slung his arm around Freddy's shoulders and led him out the door, into the cold Duluth night. "It's exactly the perfect balance of just right . . . and just a little bit nuts, Fred. I love it."

BRAINSTORMING:
Possible new names for The Peach Pit

Peachy Keen B&B

The Peach Throne

Duluth's Best Stay

Comfort to the Core

The Legend of the Three Dawns

The Black Swan

Pigs for Breakfast

Flying Pig Inn

Stone Fruit B&B

Peach Palace

THE PEACH PIT
Mordor

Pinkie's

Peachy's B&B

Family B&B

The Family Tree

The Peach Tree

 THE PEACHTREE B&B!!!!!!

HERB PEACH

INVITES YOU TO OUR 3RD GRADE

Special Person Tea

WHEN: <u>11 am Nov 23</u>

WHERE: <u>Mr. Andrus's classroom</u>

MY SPECIAL GUEST:

<u>Joye!</u>

Even though I didn't WIN the art competition (that seventh grader's mosaic portrait collection of famous women in history was AMAZING and totally deserved to win), I'm giving myself an award for having the biggest piece in the gallery. (Plus, I'm the only person who used a toilet in my art. Bonus points!)

Award for the **biggest** piece in the gallery

Freddy Peach

22

FRUITY CLUES

"It's Opening Day, whether we're ready or not," Lucy announced to her brothers and Dad over breakfast on Thanksgiving morning. The Peaches had been cleaning and organizing and rearranging and planning like crazy for the past week, and the time had come to declare they were as ready as they were going to be before the deadline. Great Aunt Lucinda's son, David, had flown into the Duluth airport that morning, and he and Great Aunt Lucinda were due at The Peachtree B&B—To check in! As actual guests!—sometime shortly after lunchtime.

"I think we're ready," Freddy declared. "Ready enough."

"Ready enough has to be good enough," Dad said, nodding.

"Your guest room is still a pit, Fred," Lucy pointed out.

Freddy shrugged. "It is what it is. I'm trying to remember to focus on what matters most, and right now, what matters most is that we have enough rooms ready for our first guests. The rest will come—eventually."

Lucy sighed. In her mind, ready enough wasn't good enough. Though her own Winter Suite and Dad and Herb's Fruit Suite were both ready to go, Freddy's guest room was still an absolute, incomplete disaster. They had all pitched in to help put it back together after they'd cleared out the bees in the wall, but even still, the third guest room had no bedding, no curtains, and no name. Freddy had been playing around with all sorts of themes and design ideas for his room—Bubble Wrap Palace (disturbing), Freshwater Aquarium (creepy), Wild West (*why?*), Medieval Dungeon (*no!*)—but had only just finalized his plans for the third suite. Playing off the theme of his Honorable Mention–winning art project, Freddy had decided to name his guest room The Treehouse Suite, with a sort of nature-and-treetop feel. He'd sketched up some designs, and Lucy could tell it was going to be cool when it was finished, but at the moment it just looked like a forest had thrown up inside their third and final guest room.

Since Freddy's guest suite wasn't yet ready, they weren't technically *done* done, but she was holding out hope that Great Aunt Lucinda and David could look past that. For most of the past few months—and their entire summer in the Peach Pie Truck—Lucy had strived for perfection with their Great Peach Experiments. But she'd finally begun to realize that perfection wasn't actually possible, nor was it necessary. She knew she had to scale back her expectations for what would be ready for their first weekend in business. They'd done what they could and it was going to have to be enough.

The dogs obviously sensed something exciting was happening, since Donny peed on the old-fashioned rug in the piano room (which he rarely did anymore), and Rudy dumped the kitchen garbage over and chewed anything with food remnants into tiny little bits that he scattered all over the floor. Herb took all four pups out for a little playtime in the yard, then locked them in the piano room for the afternoon. None of the Peaches were willing to risk letting the dogs be a part of David's B&B first impression.

After they cleaned up breakfast and the dogs' mess and set the table for that afternoon's fancy Thanksgiving feast, Dad headed off to the grocery store to stock up on a few last-minute supplies while all three kids trudged up to their bedrooms to straighten up and get dressed for Great Aunt Lucinda's arrival. Lucy kept her room neat all of the time and had already gotten dressed for the day as soon as she woke up, so she was able to spend the last few hours of downtime working on trying to solve the Hunt for Hidden Riches. She was still holding out hope that she might figure out what the map led to, and dig up some kind of treasure.

Wasn't Thanksgiving Day all about football games? So maybe this could be her Hail Mary pass into the end zone—the money they needed to finish up the rest of their projects. Or . . . maybe it would even be enough of a treasure that they could buy the Peach Pit, fair and square, and get David off their case once and for all!

But after spending the past week poring over the crudely drawn map of the Peach Pit, she was beginning to wonder if the whole map was a hoax, or some sort of prank, planted in the attic just for a laugh. *Ha-ha-ha-ha-ha*, Lucy thought bitterly. *Not at all funny*. But actually, maybe *kind of* funny? Now that she was considering this as a possibility, she was a little tempted to plant a fake treasure map for one of her brothers to find and attempt to solve. She'd get a real kick out of watching Freddy sneak around trying to find a treasure that wasn't there. But knowing Freddy, he probably *would* find a treasure, even if she hadn't hidden one anywhere. Herb, too. Both of her brothers had a knack for turning just about any-thing into something special.

As she considered this, she realized what she had to do. Much as she'd hoped to keep the Hunt for Hidden Riches a secret for her to solve alone, a way for her to fix things for her family, she had decided the time had come to involve her brothers. The time to figure this out was now or never.

"Can I talk to you for a sec?" Lucy said, poking her head inside Freddy's partially open bedroom door. He had obviously gotten distracted in the middle of his cleaning project since his room was still an utter disas-ter. "How did Herb ever share a room with you?" Lucy muttered aloud. "This is revolting."

"I'm using all this stuff." Freddy shrugged. "What's up?"

Lucy tiptoed across the room, trying to avoid the heaps of dirty socks, and LEGO blocks, and various pots of paint and torn-up paper and— "Is that a rusty pipe from one of the bathrooms?" she blurted out.

"Possibly." Freddy nudged the nasty old pipe under his bed and smiled at her. "I repeat: What's up?"

Lucy pulled the treasure map out of her pocket and set it on the bed next to her brother. "I need help solv-ing this."

Freddy studied the paper for a few seconds, his eyes

roving over all the words and details, then he looked up. "Where'd you get this?"

"That's not important," Lucy said. "It's a secret and I don't want to tell you."

Freddy nodded. Though they both had annoying moments, her brothers were almost always sensible when it came to secrets and respecting other people's privacy. "It's a map of the Peach Pit," Freddy said after ten seconds more.

"Yeah," Lucy said with an eye roll. "I know." She didn't mention that it had taken her a *bit* longer to figure that out. Maybe she should have enlisted her brothers' help sooner . . .

"Something about the way it's laid out reminds me of the dollhouse," Freddy said after another minute.

Lucy's eyes widened. *The dollhouse.* She hadn't thought of looking there. But of course—the dollhouse was an exact replica of the full-sized house. Probably *that* was where all the clues to solving this puzzle were hidden! She closed her eyes, trying not to scream. "How did you come up with that in, like, ten seconds?"

"It was more like two minutes and twenty seconds," Freddy said, grinning. "I'm slow as a sloth when it comes to cleaning. But I work fast when there's treasure on the line."

Together, Lucy and Freddy raced down two flights

of stairs to Herb's dollhouse. When they got there, Herb was organizing all the figurines and furniture inside the mini-mansion. "I'm getting everything in the Peach Pitlet ready for opening day!" Herb announced. "Wanna see?"

"Peach *Pitlet*?" Freddy laughed.

"It's what I'm calling it because it's my tiny Peach Pit," Herb explained. "Like a piglet."

Freddy grinned. "Nice. Did you know a tiny nut is called a *nutlet*? And a small pie is a *tartlet*?"

Lucy considered these words for just a second, then shook her head to get herself back on track. This information was fascinating, but so not the point. "Herb, listen, there's something we need to figure out." She showed him the map and gave him the briefest explanation possible. "If we can solve this map and find some hidden riches, it's going to erase all our problems."

"If we find a pot of money," Freddy added, his eyes getting wide, "then *we* could buy the Peach Pit from Great Aunt Lucinda. Cousin David wins, Great Aunt Lucinda wins, *and* we win."

"Exactly," Lucy said, glad to see her idea wasn't totally crazy. "So anyway, Herb, we're wondering if the dollhouse could be the key to figuring out what the map means."

Together, the three Peach kids huddled over the strange collection of boxes and numbers, looking down at the map, then gazing up into the Peach Pitlet, then back down at the map, and up again, and over and over again. "Was there *anything* in the dollhouse when I gave it to you?" Lucy asked. "Any, like, hidden panels, or secret hiding spots, or *anything* other than the few pieces of broken furniture?"

"No," Herb said, shaking his head seriously. "Nothing."

Freddy knocked at the edges of the dollhouse and tried to pry up some of the shingles, and fiddled with the floorboards inside some of the rooms.

Lucy told them about her and Maren's search for a secret safe in the house, and the dead-end Monopoly game box in the garage, and how they'd even gone so far as to poke through closets and behind bookshelves and peek under paintings. "You never know what could be hiding under art. Isn't that where rich people used to hide important things in the old days?"

"There's always cool stuff hidden in art," Freddy said. Suddenly, he went silent and held up a hand. After a long pause, he blinked and exclaimed, "There are paintings in the dollhouse!"

The other two kids leaned down for a look. "All this art was on the walls when you gave me the dollhouse!" Herb cried out. "I forgot!"

Every single room had a different piece of art with

a miniature fruit or vegetable affixed to the wall. In the space where Lucy's room would be, there was a painting of cherries; Herb's room had raspberries. On the third floor, Dad's room had something that looked like a moldy orange, The Winter Suite was wearing two paintings—one with some kind of cute tiny grapes and the other a lemon—and Freddy's room had an eggplant. There was a tomato in one second-floor guest suite, and an apple in the other. Down in the kitchen was a painting of lettuce, along with two oranges and a lime on the other walls downstairs.

Freddy ran his fingers over the apple painting in the second-floor bedroom. "Maybe if we touch the paintings in order, it will unlock some sort of magic spell and the treasure will pop out of the roof along with a bunch of confetti and lights and stuff!"

Lucy giggled. "Yeah, maybe."

Freddy looked at the map, then began to press the paintings in the rooms, one by one in order of the numbers on the map. Nothing lit up, or sparkled, or in any way indicated that they had unlocked a magic charm that would now reveal a treasure.

"Okay, plan B," Freddy said, chewing his lip.

"Could the numbers mean something else?" Lucy asked. "Like, maybe we're supposed to look at the different paintings in a special order?"

Freddy ran into his room to grab his sketchbook and a pencil. After making notes and sketches of which painting came from which room, they gently pried the paintings off the dollhouse walls and laid them out in order, according to the numbers on the map. Carefully, he wrote each of the pictures down as a list:

CHERRIES
EGGPLANT
LIME
LEMON
APPLE
RASPBERRIES
TOMATO
Some kind of orange that looks
a little rotten – O?
PEACH
PEACH
Something that kind of looks
like tiny grapes – G???
LETTUCE

"Look!" Lucy said, pointing. "The first letters of each fruit—the first six spell out CELLAR!"

"That's it!" Freddy barked out. "It's an anagram!" The dogs must have heard them cheering, since Freddy's cry set off an epic round of barking downstairs. The other two shushed him.

Herb pointed. "The rest spells out T something P P something L."

C E L L A R T (blank)
P P (something, maybe G?) L

"Cellar . . . tool?" Freddy guessed.

"But we're obviously missing a few letters, and the random Ps throw that theory out the window," Lucy pointed out.

"Wait!" Freddy said, leaning in to study the tiny paintings more carefully. "What if those aren't peaches?" He pointed at the very peach-like art that they'd pried off one of the dollhouse's first-floor walls. "They don't look fuzzy. They could be nectarines! They're super close to the same thing, but nectarines are smooth, and peaches usually have a little fur."

"Huh," Lucy said. "Okay, so maybe it's: C E L L A R T (something) N N (something) L. We need to figure out what those two weird fruits are if we want to test out this theory. But anyway, the word *cellar* doesn't really help us much, since I have no idea where we'd *find* a cellar to look. Maybe it's supposed to mean garage? Or maybe we aren't reading it right."

Herb began to say something, but suddenly the doorbell rang out down below. "They're here!" Lucy squealed. "It's David and Great Aunt Lucinda!"

"But—" Herb tried to cut in.

"What should we do?" Freddy asked. The doorbell rang again.

"Answer the door," Lucy squeaked. "We can't just let them stand out there in the cold."

"But—" Herb said again.

"Later," Lucy told him, shoving the map behind the dollhouse. "We'll have to figure it out later. Because right now . . . it's showtime!"

THE TREEHOUSE SUITE DESIGN IDEAS

23

OPEN FOR BUSINESS

Freddy thundered down the stairs alongside his siblings. He had been practicing for this moment for weeks—the arrival of their first, and most important, guests. The two people who would decide the future of The Peachtree B&B and the future of the Peach family.

As Lucy flung open the massive front door, Freddy and Herb took their places on either side of the entry-way. Freddy tucked his arms behind his back—like a guard at a fancy museum or the guys in big fluffy hats outside Buckingham Palace, where the British royal family lived—and stood straight and tall, signaling for Herb to follow suit. The moment Lucy chirped out, "Welcome!" Freddy and Herb each took a deep, gallant bow in unison.

"Wow," Great Aunt Lucinda marveled, taking a tentative step inside. "Quite the greeting." She wrapped her arm through David's and guided him past the door. "I've got to admit, it feels a little funny being a *guest* in my own darn house."

"Exactly," David muttered. "*Your* house. *Your* savings. *Your* retirement fund, if only you would sell the place."

Freddy cringed. This wasn't off to a great start. But that was okay! They could still turn things around. "Can I take your coat?" he offered, stepping forward and stretching out his arm like a coatrack. "Would you care for a refreshing beverage?"

At this, David cracked a smile. "Sure. Appreciate it." Both David and Great Aunt Lucinda handed their coats off to Freddy, who hung them up on the coatrack on the other side of the entryway, then sent Herb to fetch drinks and cookies for their guests.

Aunt Lucinda took off her hat and patted down her hair. She was wearing Freddy's favorite wig today—the one he called Purple Rain. It was a long, shimmering violet color, and it made him think of a river in an epic fantasy world. "Where are my little treasures?" she asked, craning her neck to hunt for the dogs.

"We decided it would be best if we put them away

during guest check-in," Lucy told her. "They tend to get a little overexcited when guests arrive."

"I'm sure they'll be just fine with me," Great Aunt Lucinda said, accepting the glass of lemonade and warm Welcome Cookie Herb offered each of them. "Let them out so David can spend some time with my darlings."

Freddy wasn't so sure this was a great idea, but what choice did they have? If Great Aunt Lucinda wanted to see *her* dogs in *her* house, who were they to say no?

"Are you sure?" Herb asked nervously. "Did you *see* what happened at Birch Pond?"

"Very sure," she said. "I want some quality time with my babies on their turf."

"Release the beasts!" Freddy cried out.

On his brother's command, Herb whipped open the door of the piano room. The four dogs came streaming out. They barked, jumped, and whirled around the entryway like a tornado of fur. "Dasher, Donner, Vixen, Rudolph! *Sit!*" Herb ordered.

Dash immediately did as he'd been told, but the other three pups acted as if Herb had said *Sic* rather than *Sit*. Vix leaped and pawed at the bottom of David's pant leg, nipping and tugging at it like it was a slice of ham she wanted to eat. Rudy scuttled backward and began to bark endlessly, hardly even stopping to take a breath. Donny, true to form, lifted his leg and released a stream of pee that drizzled down one side of David's suitcase.

"Come *on*," Herb groaned.

Freddy tried—but failed—to hold back a laugh. Lucy, on the other hand, was stunned into complete and utter silence.

At that exact moment, Freddy heard Dad bustling through the kitchen door. He craned his neck and could see that their dad had several large bags of food hanging off his arms. He was also cradling a hot, fresh-roasted turkey he'd ordered for their Thanksgiving dinner from the grocery store deli. Freddy's stomach rumbled at the thought of pie, stuffing, mashed potatoes, turkey with gravy, buttered rolls, and more pie. All four Peaches had been a part of their dinner preparations the past few days, but no one had wanted to handle a massive, raw turkey—so Dad had wisely ordered one from someone who actually knew how to cook something like that. They'd become breakfast and pie experts; Freddy had pointed out that they didn't need to be good at cooking *everything.*

Dad hollered out a loud *hello,* and made his way through the kitchen door into the entry hall. Dash, who had been sitting politely in the big, open space between the kitchen and the entryway, continued to do as he'd been told and did not move from his seated position.

"Dad, stop—" Herb blurted out, while Freddy continued to dream of pie. But Herb's warning came too late. Freddy watched in horror as Dad walked straight toward the statue-like, seated Dash. At the very last second, Dash popped up to save himself from getting stepped on—but got twisted up in Dad's legs while trying to get away. The collision knocked Dad off-balance. Freddy's eyes went wide as the roasted turkey flew up, up, and through the air.

It suddenly felt like life had flipped into slow motion. Freddy was pretty sure he could actually see the turkey spinning through midair. The enormous, greasy centerpiece of that afternoon's dinner sailed over Dash and Herb, then landed with a *splat!* right on David's stockinged feet.

Freddy had always thought this kind of thing only happened in movies, but it seemed he'd thought wrong. The dogs, clearly able to sniff out an easy meal, dove on the carefully wrapped turkey like a pack of hungry wolves. They chewed and tore through the bag, eager to get to the good stuff.

David pulled his feet out from under their dinner, and time flipped into fast-forward. Suddenly, everything was happening at once. While Herb and Lucy plucked the dogs up and away from their Thanksgiving dinner, Freddy grabbed David's pee-soaked suitcase (someone had to do it), and Dad dove for the turkey. "It's good to see you after all these years, David," Dad said feebly.

"Yes," David said, utterly still, obviously both shocked and horrified. "It's—uh, it's good to see you, too." Aunt Lucinda, meanwhile, shook with silent laughter.

"Well . . . welcome to The Peachtree B and B," Freddy squeaked, as soon as his siblings had gotten the last dog sealed up behind closed doors. "We do hope you'll enjoy your stay."

24

THE HUNT FOR HIDDEN RICHES

"David, please step inside your home away from home. *This* is The Fruit Suite!" Herb declared, flinging open the door to the only finished second-floor guest bedroom. He'd been rehearsing that line for weeks, and Freddy gave him a quick high five when he nailed it. While their dad hustled to put away the last of the groceries and cleaned up the turkey grease that had splattered *all* over the front entryway, the kids showed their VIP guests to their rooms so they could take some time to settle in. Herb couldn't wait to show off their fancy new B&B rooms (he just hoped they didn't ask to see Freddy's guest room *or* his personal bedroom, since they were both disaster zones)!

As David and Great Aunt Lucinda walked through the doorway of The Fruit Suite for a look, Freddy bent forward in a deep bow. *"Velcome!"* he said, in a very creepy-sounding vampire voice. Herb hadn't heard his brother try out this accent before. It was spookier than his "French" accent, for sure, but also seemed to suit the style of the house a little better.

Herb could see both of their guests marveling at the deep plum paint on the walls, the peachy accent color of all the furniture, the lemon and lime artwork decorating the walls, and the cheerful, multicolored, fruit-printed bedding. The room was an explosion of color, and it made Herb endlessly happy. He and Dad had chosen the bedding and furniture together, but Dad had let Herb pick the art posters all by himself. One of the really fun things about The Fruit Suite was you could *just* see Lake Superior if you stood on tiptoe and faced just so.

"Wow," Great Aunt Lucinda said with a smile. "This is really something." She pointed to the lemon painting on the wall. "David, do you remember I used to have a lemon painting hanging in this room, right in this very spot? Herb, you must have read the history of the walls and known just what this wall needed!"

Herb flushed with pride. "I love lemons. They're so cheerful."

Great Aunt Lucinda pointed to the framed lime art beside it. "This looks so much better here than the elderberry picture I used to have hanging on this wall. Elderberries are one of my favorite fruits and real pretty, too, but these bright limes set off the rich color of the walls perfectly."

"What's an elderberry?" Herb asked.

"They look a little like tiny red grapes," David explained. "Mom used to make us drink this horrible elderberry syrup when we were kids that she swore would keep us healthy through the long, cold Duluth winters." He made a face. "It was so sweet, I always gagged."

"But it kept you from getting sick during hockey season, didn't it?" Great Aunt Lucinda said, wagging a finger at him.

Freddy gave his brother a strange look that Herb couldn't decipher. *"Elderberries,"* Freddy whispered loudly in the direction of both his siblings. *"They look like little grapes . . ."*

"Uh . . . *huh,*" Lucy said, nodding at him like he was a little crazy.

Before Freddy could say more, David cleared his throat. "I'd appreciate it if I could take some time to get cleaned up." He cleared his throat again. "The room looks nice," he said. "I'm sure I'll be plenty comfortable."

"Okay," Lucy said quickly. "Yeah, we'll just . . . um, leave you to it! Come on downstairs when you're ready and we can get you a snack or a slice of our famous pie or find you a good book to read or—"

David cleared his throat again, cutting her off. "Thanks. I'll be down in a bit. We all have a lot to talk about. As I'm sure your dad and my mom have mentioned, I do have a buyer lined up and eager to get into the house—and us adults need to figure out what the plan is."

The three Peach kids all exchanged a look.

"Okay, yeah," Lucy choked out. "See you later, then. If you need anything, you can just push this intercom button and—"

David began to close the door. "Yes, thanks, I know. I lived here for eighteen years, remember?"

The kids and Great Aunt Lucinda made their way slowly up the central staircase to the third-floor guest suite. "Aunt Lucinda, you'll be staying in The Winter Suite," Lucy told her, pushing open the door. "I designed this space especially for you."

Herb stood beside his great aunt, watching her face as she took in all the little details Lucy had worked so hard to put in place:

- A warm, icy blue duvet cover, draped with bright red blankets and pretty, sparkly throw

pillows that made the bed look soft and
inviting
- The comfy armchair, nestled into a corner
near the window, offering a perfect view out
onto Herb's favorite part of the mansion: the
sprawling backyard
- Fluffy, off-white robes hanging from the back
of the bathroom door
- A lush, green holiday garland draped across
the top of one wall, along with a few carefully
placed vases full of Christmas tree ornaments
to make the room feel cheerful without being
too Christmas-y.

Lucy had lucked out, and the big company that had
bought Mom's solar cling invention had agreed to make
a special new design just for her (because they thought
it might be popular with other customers, too). So Lucy
was able to decorate one of the windows in The Winter
Suite with special solar clings that made it look like Jack
Frost had come for a visit and covered the window with
his icy art.

But best of all, for this room's very-first-ever guest,
his sister had somehow found and hung hundreds of
old holiday cards that Aunt Lucinda had saved over the
years. Herb's very smart sister had strung them all up

on a zigzag length of green yarn that went back and forth across the wall, so they were all waiting to welcome their great aunt home.

"Oh!" Great Aunt Lucinda said softly, stepping toward the wall. "This is marvelous." Herb noticed that Aunt Lucinda had a few tears in her eyes. "It looks just stunning, dear."

Lucy beamed back at her. "We'll give you some time to settle in and get comfortable, and then we'd love to invite you down to the living room for appetizers."

Great Aunt Lucinda pulled the three Peach kids against her in a very squishy hug. "Thank you. It's perfect."

As soon as they'd left Aunt Lucinda in her room, the kids raced back down the stairs to the dollhouse. "Did you hear that?" Herb said desperately. "It sounds like David is still planning to sell the house."

"He's not very nice," Freddy blurted out.

"I'm sure he's fine," Lucy argued. "Just kind of chilly."

Herb frowned. After spending time with Joye, he'd learned that sometimes people seem grumpy on the outside for a reason. "Don't forget that some people surprise you when you get to know them. Maybe David seems mean now, but he'll turn out nice when we get to know him."

"Maybe. He did help us solve one of the mystery

fruit paintings," Freddy said. He pointed at the miniature picture they all thought looked like tiny grapes.
"These are obviously elderberries. Great Aunt Lucinda
said she actually *had* a painting of elderberries in that
very room, back when she lived here. So that letter must
be an *E*!"

Herb grabbed Freddy's sketchbook out from behind
the dollhouse, where they'd stashed it when their
guests arrived. He pointed at the letters they'd jotted
down and changed one of the missing ones to *E*. "C
E L L A R T (something) N N E L," Herb read aloud.
Then he blurted out the information he'd been waiting
to tell his siblings since they'd first discovered the map
spelled out words: "Did you know there's a cellar under
the Peach Pit?"

"What?!" his siblings both shrieked at the same time.

Herb shushed them—David's guest room was just
steps from the stair landing!—and nodded seriously.
"I've been inside it." Herb couldn't stop himself from
grinning. *He* knew about something neither of his siblings did. So *ha* to that. But also, now *Herb* could be the
one to lead them to the treasure. "And I think I know
what the missing letter must be: *U*. I think it's supposed
to say CELLAR TUNNEL."

Freddy thwacked himself on the forehead. "Yep, that

totally makes sense. I bet that's a picture of an Ugli fruit. Proper name: Jamaican tangelo. It's a cross between a tangerine or orange with a grapefruit."

"*How* do you know that?" Lucy asked, bewildered.

Freddy tapped his forehead. "I know everything." Then he poked Herb in the ribs and said, "Wait! Are you telling us there could be a cellar tunnel under this very house?"

Herb smiled. "Follow me."

The three Peach kids headed for the stairs. But before Herb stormed down the big central staircase, he realized they couldn't go that way, since Dad was in the front entryway cleaning up the turkey glop. Eager to avoid their dad and buy a little extra time to possibly solve the Hunt for Hidden Riches, Lucy led them down into the kitchen through the twisting, tiny servant staircase.

Freddy squeaked and yipped quietly as they descended, randomly muttering things like: "Eep! I hear a mouse!" and "Yep, that's definitely tiny little pattering feet," and "If something touches me, I swear I'm going to scream."

Hearing his brother's fears voiced aloud emboldened Herb. He realized he was no longer afraid of the hidden staircases behind the walls—not anymore, not after he'd realized their house wasn't haunted. Also, he'd found and explored the hidden cellar all on his own—that took guts. And he'd written that letter to his teacher (which Mr. Andrus had said he really appreciated and promised to do better from now on!)—something that Herb felt was also pretty courageous.

Feeling brave, Herb grabbed his trusty headlamp and a few spare flashlights out of a drawer in the kitchen and led his siblings down into the cellar.

"Whoa," Lucy murmured, shining her flashlight all around as Herb led them through the dusty, chilly space under the house. He didn't stop to show off his treasure displays, or let them linger and poke around in his private fortress. He just led his siblings straight to the back of the cellar, where he'd found the strange door and dark space that he knew led to somewhere. Lucy called out, "How'd you find out this room was down here?"

"I noticed there was space under the first floor in the dollhouse," Herb said. "Then I asked Great Aunt Lucinda about it."

"Yeah, yeah," Freddy said, swiveling his flashlight into all the corners and all around his feet. "It's pretty cool down here and everything, but can you just show us to the tunnel so we can find the treasure and get out?"

Herb skipped toward the little door and twisted the knob. He pulled open the creaky wooden door and let Lucy lead the way inside the space. Herb and Freddy both cowered around their sister, peeking up and over her shoulder as Lucy shined her light into the space. "It's a tunnel, that's for sure," Lucy said softly. The walls of the tunnel were lined with more shelves, but they appeared to be empty.

"Where does it go?" Freddy asked. He stepped away from their sister just the slightest bit, and Herb could tell his brother's curiosity was stronger than his fear. Just like Herb!

"I don't know," Herb said. "I haven't actually explored back here at all."

The three kids pushed forward. The beams from all three of their flashlights were, together, bright enough to illuminate the space just enough. Herb could clearly see there were no skeletons, booby traps, or other things he needed to worry about hiding inside the mysterious tunnel. Still, he stepped carefully, just in case.

Suddenly, the beam from their lights hit a solid wall. They could go no farther. Someone, sometime in history, had sealed up the tunnel with a sheet of thick metal, creating a dead end. "This is it?" Freddy asked, obviously frustrated. "This is as far as we can go?" Herb noticed his brother looking back over his shoulder; he had a feeling Freddy was checking to make sure no one had closed the door behind them and sealed them into the tunnel like prisoners.

"Are you kidding me?" Lucy sighed. "We finally solve the map, follow it where it told us to go, and we hit a dead end?"

Freddy kicked at the dusty floor and shined his light into all the darkest corners, keeping a careful eye out for roaming mice. Lucy, meanwhile, poked and prodded at the big metal wall. "I'm trying to see if there's a button that might open a hidden door, or maybe reveal a secret keyhole."

While Herb's siblings did their thing, Herb did *his* thing and began searching the shelves around them. *His* treasures were all stored on the shelves down here in the cellar . . . maybe that's where the treasure in the Hunt for Hidden Riches would be, too. Most of the old wooden shelves were empty, having collected nothing but dust for dozens or hundreds of years. But then, on the bottommost shelf, Herb noticed something. He scrambled down onto his belly and poked an arm into the back of the space. His hand connected with something hard and cold, but whatever it was felt solid—like some kind of metal box. Herb wiggled his fingers just so, managing to turn it just enough that he could get a hold of it. He slid the box toward himself, bringing it out into the light.

It was an old, rusty metal box with *Star Wars* characters printed on the outside.

Herb gasped, which was enough to get his siblings' attention. "What is that?" Freddy asked, spinning around.

"I think it's an antique lunch box," Lucy said.

"Or," Herb said, smiling, "we just found our treasure."

25

THE MYSTERIOUS (LUNCH) BOX

"Open it!" Lucy cried. She couldn't believe they were this close . . . could this actually be the hidden riches she'd been searching for all this time? Hidden away in a rusty old lunch box? That was okay; Lucy knew fun things came in all kinds of packages. "Come on, Herbie."

Her little brother popped the metal tabs on one side of the box and the lid squeaked open. Inside, they found:

- A Matchbox car
- Some pieces of very old and stale saltwater taffy (Freddy unwrapped and tried to bite into one, just to check)
- A postcard from Kure Beach (the exact same North Carolina town the Peaches had spent a week in that very summer!)

- A little leather pouch with colorful rocks and some chunks of very fake-looking gold
- Some sort of red fur blob (that Freddy informed her was something called a lucky rabbit's foot—*ew!*)
- A Duluth newspaper from 1987 that said TWINS WIN!!! on the front cover

"What *is* all this?" Lucy asked, poking through the box.

"And where's the cash?" Freddy said. "Or gold, or jewels, or . . . *riches?*"

Herb poked his tongue out of the corner of his mouth, and Lucy could tell he was doing mental math. "If this newspaper is from 1987, I think Dad and David probably would have been around Lucy's age when this newspaper came out." He looked up at his siblings, his eyes wide. "Guys, what if this is some sort of time capsule?"

"That'd be cool," Freddy said. "But an old newspaper and some shiny rocks aren't going to help us buy this house."

"Yeah." Lucy nodded. "But since we found it, and there doesn't seem to be any *other* riches hidden down here, we might as well bring this upstairs and see if Dad or David has ever seen any of this stuff."

The trio trudged upstairs and went in through the kitchen door. The house smelled warm and homey, like pie spices and fresh-baked bread (and, mysterious as always, a little like split pea soup). Lucy looked around, smiling, when she spotted her dad dancing in from the dining room wearing his TRUST ME, I'M A SCIENTIST apron. He was singing along to music that was only playing in his head, and he looked happy and content.

Lucy didn't want to give up the Peach Pit. She loved living here, and she was excited to share their beautiful B&B with strangers. They'd turned Great Aunt Lucinda's old money pit of a mansion into a home—*their* home—and it wasn't fair that David was trying to sell it out from under them. Just because they hadn't finished everything by the deadline, it wasn't right that he would hand it off to the highest bidder!

But, Lucy reasoned, it also wasn't fair that they were just *taking* it from Great Aunt Lucinda. Lucy wished there were some way for *everyone* to win in this scenario. But with no hidden treasure buried in the cellar tunnel to save them, the Peaches had no money and no time left to figure out a creative solution.

"Dad," Herb called, rushing toward their father. "Look what we found in the cellar!"

"The cellar?" Dad said, wiping his hands on his apron.

"You guys found the cellar, huh?" David asked, strolling into the kitchen like he owned the place. In a way, Lucy realized, he kind of *did*. He was Great Aunt Lucinda's son, which meant this place should have and could have been his. So it made sense that he wanted her to sell it and make some money, probably so that someday *he* could inherit a big pile of cash that he would probably use for something dumb.

"I found the cellar after that last summer you stayed with us," David told Dad, settling into a seat at the counter. "It's this awesome hidey-hole under the house. I was so excited to show it to you, but you didn't come back to stay with us the next summer, so I never got a chance to take you down there."

"Yeah," Dad said with a sigh. "My dad and I spent that next summer moving to a new military base, remember? He wanted me to start classes earlier than usual that fall to get a head start at my new school." Lucy watched Dad's face as he said this. She could tell that hadn't been a good year of Dad's life.

David grabbed a cookie out of Great Aunt Lucinda's old ceramic chicken cookie jar and took a bite. "Yum," he said, nodding. "These are absolutely delicious. If your breakfast is half as tasty as your Welcome Cookies, you guys really *can* bake."

"Thanks," Freddy said. "It's my own recipe.

Sometimes I add pretzels or chocolate-hazelnut spread or a couple other things—I usually take notes while I'm making them, but I can't remember exactly what was in this batch. They're not perfect yet, but I don't really mind experimenting with new recipes once or twice a week. It will keep things from getting boring at the B and B . . ." He trailed off, then added in a softer voice, ". . . if we get to stay, that is."

Aunt Lucinda strolled into the kitchen then, joining the rest of the family as they stood around the food mess that would soon be part of a beautiful afternoon meal.

"So, what did you find down in this cellar?" Dad asked, gesturing for Herb to hand over the lunch box. "Oh, geez, Dave—that looks like your old *Star Wars* lunch box!"

Both David and Dad began to laugh. David said, "Man, did I love that lunch box. I bet I could sell this for a few hundred bucks. It must be a collector's item by now!" Then he shook his head. "But I would never get rid of it. This thing was my most prized possession."

Herb placed the lunch box carefully on the counter and popped open the tabs. When he opened it, David gasped. "Oh wow, I forgot about this!" Together, David and Dad pulled all the items out of the metal box and set them out on the counter.

"This was the car we were always fighting over that summer we drove up to Canada!" Dad exclaimed, pulling the Matchbox car out of the tin. He grinned at David and said, "You told me it got lost!"

David shrugged. "Or I hid it, because I was tired of fighting you for it. Mom always took your side and told me I should share the best stuff with our guest." He laughed.

Great Aunt Lucinda pointed to him, nodding. "That is absolutely true! You never take the best toys for yourself at your own house. You should always share them with your guest, since *you* can use them anytime, but your guest only gets a short while with them."

"Yeah," David said. "When I found the car hidden at the very bottom of my desk a few years later, I felt bad about hiding it from you—so I was planning to give it to you." He looked up at the kids and asked, "How did you find this stuff, exactly?"

Lucy pulled the map out of her pocket and explained how she'd been following the Hunt for Hidden Riches. "We finally figured out that the clues on the map matched up with clues in the dollhouse, and it led us down to the cellar tunnel. We found this old box on a shelf way at the back."

David closed his eyes and whistled. "Yep, that's

exactly where I hid it. Probably close to thirty years ago, now."

Herb held up the newspaper and said, "At least thirty-five years ago. This newspaper is from 1987."

"Geez," David whistled. "I kind of forget I'm that old."

"So *you* hid this box?" Lucy asked him.

"Yep," David said, zipping the Matchbox car back and forth across the kitchen counter. "I wanted to figure out a fun way to lead your dad down into the cellar. So I made, like, a time capsule of some of our favorite things from the summer trips we'd taken together, and then I planted clues as art in the dollhouse, since we loved playing with that thing. Then I made that map, and I was going to have Wally spend the next summer trying to figure it out."

"But Dad never came back to Duluth for the summer," Freddy said.

"Nope," Dad agreed. "Not until I was a lot older, and Dave was in college—"

David cut him off to say, "And I'd forgotten all about having hidden this down there by then. I can't believe you guys found it."

"What's the deal with that tunnel?" Freddy asked. "Where does it go? And why is it blocked off?"

Aunt Lucinda said, "I don't know for sure, but there was a rumor that one of Duluth's early millionaires owned both *this* house and the house next door. He put in a tunnel between them so he could shuttle his stuff— or himself—back and forth without people seeing him. Or maybe so he could hide his most valuable possession down there? I don't know if those theories and rumors are true, but I like the story so I kept it."

"So, the tunnel just goes to the house next door?" Herb verified. "Not, like, a secret haunted pit of doom or a room full of snakes or Jabba the Hut's lair or something?"

Freddy snickered as though Herb were being totally ridiculous. Lucy wanted to remind him that *he* had been a total wimp about *mice* in the basement just twenty minutes before, but she decided not to bring it up.

"Yep. The only place that tunnel leads is to the house next door," Aunt Lucinda told them. "And it got blocked off halfway between the two houses before we bought it. So now it's more of a long cave than a tunnel. Kind of neat anyway, don't you think?"

"Very neat," Lucy agreed.

"What are the rest of the treasures in the box?" Herb asked eagerly, bending over the pile of random stuff on the counter.

"This was your favorite taffy place out in North Carolina, remember?" David said, grabbing a piece of taffy as he smiled up at Dad. "When we got home from our trip out there that last summer, I saved all the grape pieces in my stash for you—since they were your favorite. They're probably not all that good anymore."

"They're not," Freddy confirmed. "I checked."

Dad and David spent the next few minutes reminiscing over more old memories and favorite things from their summers together—the colorful rocks and gold pieces they'd collected during a trip out to the Badlands and Black Hills in South Dakota; the postcard bought at the amusement park during their last summer trip together to Kure Beach; the lucky rabbit's foot that they'd bought together at a gift shop during a trip to Michigan's Upper Peninsula that they *swore* brought them good luck the rest of the summer; the newspaper that came out after David's favorite baseball team—the Minnesota Twins—won the World Series against Dad's childhood favorite, the St. Louis Cardinals.

By the time they'd finished talking about all the stuff that had been tucked inside David's old lunch box, Lucy's attitude about David had totally shifted. He actually seemed really nice, and she had to admit that it took a special sort of person to set up a whole treasure hunt for someone else. A treasure hunt that led to a box full of favorite things, no less!

Lucy decided the time was right for her to say what she knew she needed to say. Because the Peaches were special, too, and she hated that David was trying to take this precious home—and the chance to create even more happy memories like this—away from them. There was no time like the present, and David was obviously in a warm-and-fuzzy mood. "Listen," she said, her voice cracking. "Before dinner, I just wanted to say that we love this house. I know you have someone who wants to buy it, and that it would probably be easiest and more sensible to sell it to someone who can pay a lot of money for it, but we've worked really hard to turn this place into a gorgeous B and B and we just want a chance to—"

"We can't sell it," David blurted out.

"What?" Lucy, Herb, and Freddy all said together.

Dad just blinked, clearly surprised at what had just plopped out of his cousin's mouth.

David shook his head. "Mom and I have been talking about it a lot. She's been slowly winning me over. And now that I'm actually here, remembering all this history that's hidden deep inside the house, I know she's right. You're all right. There's just too much history in this house for us to give it up; it's a treasure. I want a home base that I can visit when I come back through Minnesota, and if we sell this place, I'll have to stay in some random, impersonal hotel. Why would I want to do that, when I could stay at The Peachtree B and B and feel like I'm coming home?"

"So . . ." Lucy began. She swallowed. "We get to stay?"

"On one condition," David said seriously.

"What's that?" Dad asked.

"I just want to know that there's always a place for me here," David said. "It feels good to be home and to spend some time with family. Even though I don't want to live in Duluth anymore, it sure is nice to be surrounded by all these memories and feel like a part of your family. We've had a lot of great times in this house, and I know your family will continue them."

Aunt Lucinda wrapped her arm around him.

"Mom made the right choice when she decided to share it with you all," David said. "So, let's make this work. I'd be happy to offer up some money as an investor if you need any more cash to finish projects up. In exchange, I'd expect to stay for free when I come back to visit at Christmas. Do we have a deal?"

Dad looked to Lucy, Freddy, Herb, and Great Aunt

Lucinda, then grinned. "David, we have a deal. Your room will always be ready for you."

Aunt Lucinda nodded. "Excellent news. Then that's settled."

"And in other excellent news, dinner's ready," Dad announced. He cringed. "Except I feel I must remind you, there will be no turkey on the table this year."

"Who needs turkey?" Great Aunt Lucinda said. "Since we're throwing sensible out the window today, I say we should start this meal with pie."

Lucy couldn't agree more.

Please rate The Peachtree B&B!
10 = SUPER 1 = THE WORST

OVERALL HAPPINESS OF YOUR STAY
1   2   3   4   5   6   7   8   9   (10)

GUEST ROOM COMFORT
1   2   3   4   5   6   7   8   9   (10)

FOOD
1   2   3   4   5   6   7   8   9   (10)

SERVICE
1   2   3   4   5   6   7   8   9   (10)

OTHER COMMENTS:

I absolutely loved staying at what is surely
Duluth's finest B&B! The highlights include:

- All the personal touches throughout this lovely
  home (so much history in one magnificent house!)
- The friendly (and charming) staff
- Delicious food (and a peach pie that I must get
  the recipe for!)

- Adorable BEB pets (even if those little
  monsters did de-stuff my pillows . . .)

I can't wait to visit your wonderful home again.
In the meantime, I'll tell all my friends to book their
stay! Do you offer Friends & Family discounts?

Much love,
Your Great Aunt Lucinda

ERIN SODERBERG DOWNING has written more than fifty books for kids, tweens, and young adults, including several series for young readers: The Great Peach Experiment (a Junior Library Guild Gold Standard Selection), Puppy Pirates, The Quirks, and Disney's Daring Dreamers Club. She has also published many other novels for middle-grade readers, including *Moon Shadow* and *Controlled Burn*. Erin's favorite hobbies are reading, swimming, baking, exploring the woods, traveling with her family, and walking around Minneapolis lakes with her fluffy and mischievous dogs, Wally and Nutmeg. More information can be found at www.erinsoderberg.com.